Whereyouwantogoto
AND
Other Unlikely Tales

E. NESBIT

❖ ❖

Whereyouwantogoto
AND
Other Unlikely Tales

Illustrated by
H. R. MILLAR
and
CLAUDE A. SHEPPERSON

Edited by Jonathan Cott

BAREFOOT BOOKS
Boston & Bath
1993

Barefoot Books
an imprint of
Shambhala Publications, Inc.
Horticultural Hall
300 Massachusetts Avenue
Boston, Massachusetts 02115

Barefoot Books Ltd
P.O. Box 95
Kingswood, Bristol 5BH

9 8 7 6 5 4 3 2 1

First Barefoot Books Edition

Cover art rendered in color
by Elizabeth Hope Shaw
Series designed by Dede Cummings/IPA
Printed in China on acid-free paper ∞

Distributed in the United States by
Random House, Inc., and in Canada
by Random House of Canada Ltd

See page 206 for Library of Congress
Cataloging-in-Publication data.

CONTENTS

*The Cockatoucan
or Great Aunt Willoughby*
1

*Whereyouwantogoto
or the Bouncible Ball*
55

*The Prince, Two Mice,
and Some Kitchen-Maids*
97

*Melisande
or Long and Short Division*
133

*The Town in the Library
in the Town in the Library*
173

❖ ❖

Editor's Preface

ONCE UPON A TIME, children's story books would, as a matter of course, describe the misdeeds of mischievous and disobedient little boys and girls, whose antisocial behavior always merited and resulted in some appropriate rebuke or punishment. (A famous, if extreme, example of this type of book, *Slovenly Peter,* showed a child who played with matches incinerating himself.) In contrast to such a breach of discipline, these stories would inevitably extol the saving virtues of dutifulness, moderation, self-control, rationality, prudence, and industry. At the end of the Victorian and the beginning of the Edwardian periods, however, there was an author—still popular today—who devoted her life to writing children's books that unwaveringly and enthusiastically took the side of the children *themselves*.

E. (for Edith) Nesbit (1858–1924) was a remarkable bohemian woman who grew up as a tomboy, had bobbed hair, wore loose "aesthetic" dress (and pantaloons for bicycling), flaunted scores of silver bangles on her arms, and rolled and smoked her own cigarettes. She and her husband, the journalist Hubert Bland, were founding members of the Fabian Society, and lived in a large moated house in Eltham, Kent, that served as a kind of combination salon/commune where writers, painters, politicians, poor relations, illegitimate children, waifs, and cranks of all stripes used to congregate. One of Edith's friends would later recall the then 32-year-old author with her "tall, lithe, boyish-girl figure" and "a comradely frankness of manner, which made me at once feel that I had known her all my life. . . . She suggested adventure, playing truant, robbing orchards, or even running away to sea." Edith Nesbit herself once confessed to having remained a child in a grown-up world, "trusting to the verge of what a real grown-up would call imbecility"; and she added: "If these children, disguised by grown-up bodies, are ever recognized for what they are, it is when they happen to have the use of their pens—when they write for and about children."

Nesbit is best known for her books about the six clever, rambunctious

Bastable children (*The Story of the Treasure Seekers, The Wouldbegoods,* and others) and fantasy novels like *Five Children and It, The Phoenix and the Carpet,* and *The Story of the Amulet,* which introduced the Psammead, one of the author's most inspired characters—a wish-granting sand fairy with bat's ears and snail's eyes.

Less well known, but among Nesbit's greatest work, are her wonder tales and fairy tales in which she plays with, satirizes, and embraces the conventions of these genres, enabling her to bring together and meld her gifts as a brilliant humorist, social critic, and narrative prestidigitator.

"Perhaps it was because E. Nesbit remained emotionally about twelve years old all her life," writes the novelist Alison Lurie (and one of Nesbit's greatest admirers), "that she found it natural to speak as one intelligent child to another, in a tone now so common in juvenile fiction that it is hard to realize how radical and even shocking it would have seemed at the time." When Matilda, the little girl in the Nesbit story "The Cockatoucan," for example, objects to visiting her great-aunt Willoughby, she knows exactly why:

> She would be asked about her lessons, and how many marks she had, and whether she had been a good girl. I can't think why grown-up people don't see how impertinent these questions are. Suppose you were to answer, "I'm top of my class, Auntie, thank you, and I'm very good. And now let's have a little talk about you. Aunt, dear, how much money have you got, and have you been scolding the servants

again, or have you tried to be good and patient as a properly brought-up aunt should be, eh, dear?"

In "Whereyouwantogoto," the title story of this book, two children, Selim and Thomasina, start bouncing along with their magic Bouncible Ball through city, suburb, and field until they reach the land of Whereyouwantogoto—a pristine Eden of sea, sand, rocks, caves, and uncorrupted nature; where there were "no bathing machines or bands, no nursemaids or policemen or aunts or uncles," where days passed like a happy dream, "only broken by surprising and delightful meals." In this land where nothing was "wrong" as long as you were "good," the two children, unable to leave something wonderful enough alone, destroy their paradise by sum-

moning up a housemaid and policeman and turning Whereyouwantogoto
into a tacky seaside resort. For being
"bad"—lacking imagination—Selim
and Thomasina are cast out of Eden,
as if—E. Nesbit seems to suggest—
there were an underlying, inescapable
power in human consciousness that
makes us fall back onto conventional
values and behavior. But in her stories,
the author makes us understand—just
as the heroine in "Melisande" learns
for herself—that one is not happy because one is good, but good because
one is happy.

It is a notion that is still worth con-
sidering.

The stories in this collection were
first published in 1901 under the title
Nine Unlikely Tales. The original illus-

trations by H. R. Millar and Claude A. Shepperson are included here.

JONATHAN COTT
Series Editor

Whereyouwantogoto
AND
Other Unlikely Tales

The Cockatoucan

OR GREAT AUNT WILLOUGHBY

M ALTIDA'S ears were red and shiny. So were her cheeks. Her hands were red too. This was because Pridmore had washed her. It was not the usual washing, which makes you clean and comfortable, but the "thorough good wash," which makes you burn and smart till you wish you could be like the poor little savages who do not know anything, and run about bare in the sun, and only go into the water when they are hot.

Matilda wished she could have been

born in a savage tribe instead of at Brixton.

"Little savages," she said, "don't have their ears washed thoroughly, and they don't have new dresses that are prickly in the insides round their arms, and cut them round the neck. Do they, Pridmore?"

But Pridmore only said, "Stuff and nonsense," and then she said, "don't wriggle so, child, for goodness' sake."

Pridmore was Matilda's nursemaid. Matilda sometimes found her trying. Matilda was quite right in believing that savage children do not wear frocks that hurt. It is also true that savage children are not over-washed, over-brushed, over-combed, gloved, booted, and hatted and taken in an omnibus to Streatham to see their Great-aunt Willoughby. This was intended to be Matilda's fate. Her mother had arranged it. Pridmore had prepared her for it. Matilda, knowing resistance to be vain, had submitted to it.

But Destiny had not been consulted, and Destiny had plans of its own for Matilda.

When the last button of Matilda's boots had been fastened (the button-hook always had a nasty temper, especially when it was hurried, and that day it bit a little piece of Matilda's leg quite spitefully) the wretched child was taken downstairs and put on a chair in the hall to wait while Pridmore popped her own things on.

"I shan't be a minute," said Pridmore. Matilda knew better. She seated herself to wait, and swung her legs miserably. She had been to her Great-aunt Willoughby's before, and she knew exactly what to expect. She

Matilda swung her legs miserably.

would be asked about her lessons, and how many marks she had, and whether she had been a good girl. I can't think why grown-up people don't see how impertinent these questions are. Suppose you were to answer, "I'm top of my class, Auntie, thank you, and I'm very good. And now let's have a little talk about you. Aunt, dear, how much money have you got, and have you been scolding the servants again, or have you tried to be good and patient as a properly brought up aunt should be, eh, dear?"

Try this method with one of your aunts next time she begins asking you questions, and write and tell me what she says.

Matilda knew exactly what the Aunt Willoughby's questions would be, and she knew how, when they were answered, her aunt would give her a small biscuit with carraway seeds in it, and then tell her to go with Pridmore and have her hands and face washed again.

Then she would be sent to walk in the garden—the garden had a gritty path, and geraniums and calceolarias and lobelias in the beds. You might not pick anything. There would be minced veal at dinner, with three-cornered bits of toast round the dish, and a tapioca pudding. Then the long afternoon with a book, a bound volume of the "Potterer's Saturday Night"—nasty small print—and all the stories about children who died young because they were too good for this world.

Matilda wriggled wretchedly. If she had been a little less uncomfortable she would have cried, but her new frock was too tight and prickly to let her forget it for a moment even in tears.

When Pridmore came down at last, she said, "Fie, for shame! What a sulky face!"

And Matilda said, "I'm not."

"Oh, yes you are," said Pridmore, "you know you are, you don't appreciate your blessings."

"I wish it was your Aunt Willoughby," said Matilda.

"Nasty, spiteful little thing!" said Pridmore, and she shook Matilda.

Then Matilda tried to slap Pridmore, and the two went down the steps not at all pleased with each other. They went down the dull road to the dull omnibus, and Matilda was crying a little.

Now Pridmore was a very careful person, though cross, but even the most careful persons make mistakes sometimes—and she must have taken the wrong omnibus, or this story could never have happened, and where should we all have been then? This shows you that even mistakes are sometimes valuable, so do not be hard on grown-up people if they are wrong sometimes. You know after all, it hardly ever happens.

It was a very bright green and gold omnibus, and inside the cushions were green and very soft. Matilda and her nursemaid had it all to themselves, and Matilda began to feel more comfortable, especially as she had wriggled till she had burst one of her shoulder-seams and got more room for herself inside her frock.

So she said, "I'm sorry I was cross, Priddy dear."

Pridmore said, "So you ought to be." But she never said *she* was sorry for being cross. But you must not expect grown-up people to say that.

It was certainly the wrong omnibus because instead of jolting slowly along dusty streets, it went quickly and smoothly down a green lane, with flowers in the hedges, and green trees overhead. Matilda was so delighted that she sat quite still, a very rare thing with her. Pridmore was reading a penny story called "The Vengeance of the Lady Constantia," so she did not notice anything.

"I don't care. I shan't tell her," said Matilda, "she'd stop the 'bus as likely as not."

At last the 'bus stopped of its own accord. Pridmore put her story in her pocket and began to get out.

"Well, I never!" she said, and got out very quickly and ran round to where the horses were. They were white horses with green harness, and their tails were very long indeed.

"Hi, young man!" said Pridmore to the omnibus driver, "you've brought us to the wrong place. This isn't Streatham Common, this isn't."

The driver was the most beautiful omnibus driver you ever saw, and his clothes were like him in beauty. He had white silk stockings and a ruffled silk shirt of white, and his coat and breeches were green and gold. So was the three-cornered hat which he lifted very politely when Pridmore spoke to him.

"I fear," he said kindly, "that you must have taken, by some unfortunate misunderstanding, the wrong omnibus."

"When does the next go back?"

"The omnibus does not go back. It

runs from Brixton here once a month, but it doesn't go back."

"But how does it get to Brixton again, to start again, I mean," asked Matilda.

"We start a new one every time," said the driver, raising his three-cornered hat once more.

"And what becomes of the old ones?" Matilda asked.

"Ah," said the driver, smiling, "that depends. One never knows beforehand, things change so nowadays. Good morning. Thank you so much for your patronage. No, on no account, Madam."

He waved away the eightpence which Pridmore was trying to offer him for the fare from Brixton, and drove quickly off.

When they looked round them, no, this was certainly not Streatham

He waved away the eightpence.

Common. The wrong omnibus had brought them to a strange village—the neatest, sweetest, reddest, greenest, cleanest, prettiest village in the world. The houses were grouped round a village green, on which children in pretty loose frocks or smocks were playing happily.

Not a tight armhole was to be seen, or even imagined in that happy spot. Matilda swelled herself out and burst three hooks and a bit more of the shoulder seam.

The shops seemed a little queer, Matilda thought. The names somehow did not match the things that were to be sold. For instance, where it said "Elias Groves, Tinsmith," there were loaves and buns in the window, and the shop that had "Baker" over the door, was full of perambulators—the grocer and the wheelwright seemed to have changed names, or shops, or something—and Miss Skimpling, Dressmaker or Milliner, had her shop window full of pork and sausage meat.

"What a funny, nice place," said Matilda. "I am glad we took the wrong omnibus."

A little boy in a yellow smock had come up close to them.

"I beg your pardon," he said very politely, 'but all strangers are brought before the king at once. Please follow me."

"Well, of all the impudence," said Pridmore. "Strangers, indeed! And who may you be, I should like to know?"

"I," said the little boy, bowing very low, "am the Prime Minister. I know I do not look it, but appearances are deceitful. It's only for a short time. I shall probably be myself again by to-morrow.''

Pridmore muttered something which the little boy did not hear. Matilda caught a few words. "Smacked," "bed," "bread and water"—familiar words all of them.

"If it's a game," said Matilda to the boy, "I should like to play."

He frowned.

"I advise you to come at once," he said, so sternly that even Pridmore was a little frightened. "His Majesty's Palace is in this direction." He walked away, and Matilda made a sudden jump, dragged her hand out of Pridmore's, and ran after him. So Pridmore had to follow, still grumbling.

The Palace stood in a great green park dotted with white-flowered may-bushes. It was not at all like an English palace, St. James's or Buckingham Pal-

ace, for instance, because it was very
beautiful and very clean. When they
got in they saw that the Palace was
hung with green silk. The footmen
had green and gold liveries, and all the
courtiers' clothes were the same col-
ours.

Matilda and Pridmore had to wait a
few moments while the King changed
his sceptre and put on a clean crown,
and then they were shown into the
Audience Chamber. The King came
to meet them.

"It is kind of you to have come so
far," he said. "Of *course* you'll stay at
the Palace?" He looked anxiously at
Matilda.

"Are you *quite* comfortable, my
dear?" he asked doubtfully.

Matilda was very truthful—for a
girl.

"No," she said, "my frock cuts me round the arms—"

"Ah," said he, "and you brought no luggage—some of the Princess's frocks—her old ones perhaps—yes—yes—this person—your maid, no doubt?"

A loud laugh rang suddenly through the hall. The King looked uneasily round, as though he expected something to happen. But nothing seemed likely to occur.

"Yes," said Matilda, "Pridmore is—Oh, dear!"

For before her eyes she saw an awful change taking place in Pridmore. In an instant all that was left of the original Pridmore were the boots and the hem of her skirt—the top part of her had changed into painted iron and glass, and even as Matilda looked the bit of skirt that was left got flat and

The top part of Pridmore changed into painted iron and glass.

hard and square. The two feet turned into four feet, and they were iron feet, and there was no more Pridmore.

"Oh, my poor child," said the King, "your maid has turned into an Automatic Machine."

It was too true. The maid had turned into a machine such as those which you see in a railway station— greedy, grasping things which take your pennies and give you next to nothing in chocolate and no change.

But there was no chocolate to be seen through the glass of the machine that once had been Pridmore. Only little rolls of paper.

The King silently handed some pennies to Matilda. She dropped one into the machine and pulled out the little drawer. There was a scroll of paper. Matilda opened it and read—

"Don't be tiresome."

She tried again. This time it was—

"If you don't give over I'll tell your Ma first thing when she comes home."

The next was—

"Go along with you do—always worrying;" so then Matilda *knew*.

"Yes," said the King sadly, "I fear there's no doubt about it. Your maid has turned into an Automatic Nagging Machine. Never mind, my dear, she'll be all right to-morrow."

"I like her best like this, thank you," said Matilda quickly. "I needn't put in any more pennies, you see."

"Oh, we mustn't be unkind and neglectful," said the King gently, and he dropped in a penny. *He* got—

"You tiresome boy, you. Leave me be this minute."

"I can't help it," said the King wearily; "you've no idea how suddenly things change here. It's because—but I'll tell you all about it at tea-time. Go with nurse now, my dear, and see if any of the Princess's frocks will fit you."

Then a nice, kind, cuddly nurse led Matilda away to the Princess's apartments, and took off the stiff frock that hurt, and put on a green silk gown, as soft as birds' breasts, and Matilda kissed her for sheer joy at being so comfortable.

"And now, dearie," said the nurse, "you'd like to see the Princess, wouldn't you? Take care you don't hurt yourself with her. She's rather sharp."

Matilda did not understand this then. Afterwards she did.

The nurse took her through many marble corridors and up and down many marble steps, and at last they came to a garden full of white roses, and in the middle of it, on a green satin-covered eiderdown, as big as a feather bed, sat the Princess in a white gown.

She got up when Matilda came towards her, and it was like seeing a yard and a half of white tape stand up on one end and bow—a yard and a half of broad white tape, of course; but what is considered broad for tape is very narrow indeed for princesses.

"How are you?" said Matilda, who had been taught manners.

"Very slim indeed, thank you," said the Princess. And she was. Her face was so white and thin that it looked as though it were made of an oyster-shell. Her hands were thin and white, and her fingers reminded Matilda of fish-bones. Her hair and eyes were black, and Matilda thought she might

The princess was like a yard and a half of white tape.

have been pretty if she had been fatter. When she shook hands with Matilda her bony fingers hurt quite hard.

The Princess seemed pleased to see her visitor, and invited her to sit with Her Highness on the satin cushion.

"I have to be very careful or I should break," said she; "that's why the cushion is so soft, and I can't play many games for fear of accidents. Do you know any sitting-down games?"

The only thing Matilda could think of was Cat's-cradle, so they played that with the Princess's green hair-ribbon. Her fish-bony fingers were much cleverer than Matilda's little fat, pink paws.

Matilda looked about her between the games and admired everything very much, and asked questions, of course. There was a very large bird chained to a perch in the middle of a very large cage. Indeed the cage was so big that it took up all one side of the rose-garden. The bird had a yellow crest like a cockatoo and a very large bill like a toucan. (If you do not know what a toucan is you do not deserve ever to go to the Zoological Gardens again.)

"What is that bird?" asked Matilda.

"Oh," said the Princess, "that's my pet Cockatoucan; he's very valuable. If he were to die or be stolen the Green Land would wither up and grow like New Cross or Islington."

"How horrible!" said Matilda.

"I've never been to those places, of course," said the Princess, shuddering, "but I hope I know my geography."

"All of it?" asked Matilda.

"Even the exports and imports," said the Princess. "Goodbye, I'm so thin I have to rest a good deal or I should wear myself out. Nurse, take her away."

So nurse took her away to a wonderful room, where she amused herself till tea-time with all the kind of toys that you see and want in the shop when some one is buying you a box of bricks or a puzzle map—the kind of toys you never get because they are so expensive.

Matilda had tea with the King. He was full of true politeness and treated Matilda exactly as though she had been grown up—so that she was extremely happy and behaved beautifully.

The King told her all his troubles.

"You see," he began, "what a pretty place my Green Land was once. It has points even now. But things aren't what they used to be. It's that bird, that Cockatoucan. We daren't kill it or give it away. And every time it laughs something changes. Look at my Prime Minister. He was a six-foot man. And look at him now. I could lift him with one hand. And then your poor maid. It's all that bad bird."

"Why *does* it laugh?" asked Matilda.

"I can't think," said the King; "I can't see anything to laugh at."

"Can't you give it lessons, or something nasty to make it miserable?"

"I have, I do, I assure you, my dear child. The lessons that bird has to swallow would choke a Professor."

"Does it eat anything else besides lessons?"

"Christmas pudding. But there— what's the use of talking—that bird would laugh if it were fed on dog biscuits."

His Majesty sighed and passed the buttered toast.

"You can't possibly," he went on, "have any idea of the kind of things that happen. That bird laughed one day at a Cabinet Council, and all my ministers turned into little boys in yellow socks. And we can't get any laws made till they come right again. It's not their fault, and I must keep their situations open for them, of course, poor things."

"Of course," said Matilda.

"There was a Dragon, now," said the King. "When he came I offered the Princess's hand and half my kingdom to any one who would kill him. It's an offer that is always made, you know."

"Yes," said Matilda.

"Well, a really respectable young Prince came along, and every one turned out to see him fight the Dragon. As much as ninepence each was paid for the front seats, I assure you. The trumpet sounded and the Dragon came hurrying up. A trumpet is like a dinner-bell to a Dragon, you know. And the Prince drew his bright sword and we all shouted, and then that wretched bird laughed and the Dragon turned into a pussy-cat, and the Prince killed it before he could stop himself. The populace was furious."

"What happened then?" asked Matilda.

"Well, I did what I could. I said, 'You shall marry the Princess just the same.' So I brought the Prince home, and when we got there the Cockatoucan had just been laughing again, and the Princess had turned into a very old German governess. The Prince went home in a great hurry and an awful temper. The Princess was all right in a day or two. These are trying times, my dear."

"I am so sorry for you," said Matilda, going on with the preserved ginger.

"Well you may be," said the miserable Monarch; "but if I were to try to tell you all that that bird has brought on my poor kingdom I should keep you up till long past your proper bedtime."

"I don't mind," said Matilda kindly. "Do tell me some more."

"Why," the King went on, growing now more agitated, "why, at one titter from that revolting bird the long row of ancestors on my Palace wall grew red-faced and vulgar; they began to drop their H's and to assert that their name was Smith from Clapham Junction."

"How dreadful!"

"And once," said the King in a whimper, "it laughed so loudly that two Sundays came together and next Thursday got lost, and went prowling away and hid itself on the other side of Christmas."

"And now," he said suddenly, "it's bedtime."

"Must I go?" asked Matilda.

"Yes please," said the King. "I tell all strangers this tragic story because I always feel that perhaps some stranger might be clever enough to help me. You seem a very nice little girl. Do you think you are clever?"

It is very nice even to be *asked* if you are clever. Your Aunt Willoughby knows well enough that you are not. But kings do say nice things. Matilda was very pleased.

"I don't think I am clever," she was saying quite honestly, when suddenly the sound of a hoarse laugh rang through the banqueting hall. Matilda put her hands to her head.

"Oh, dear!" she cried, "I feel so different. Oh! wait a minute. Oh! whatever is it? Oh!"

Then she was silent for a moment. Then she looked at the King and said, "I was wrong, your Majesty, I *am* clever, and I know it is not good for me to sit up late. Goodnight. Thank you so much for your nice party. In the morning I think I shall be clever enough to help you, unless the bird laughs me back into the other kind of Matilda."

But in the morning Matilda's head felt strangely clear; only when she came down to breakfast full of plans for helping the King, she found that the Cockatoucan must have laughed in the night, for the beautiful Palace had turned into a butcher's shop, and the King, who was too wise to fight against Fate, had tucked up his royal robes, and was busy in the shop weighing out six ounces of the best mutton-chops for a child with a basket.

"I don't know how ever you can help me now," he said, despairingly; "as long as the Palace stays like this, it's no use trying to go on with being a king, or anything. I can only try to be a good butcher. You shall keep the accounts if you like, till that bird laughs me back into my Palace again."

So the King settled down to business, respected by his subjects, who had all, since the coming of the Cockatoucan, had their little ups and downs. And Matilda kept the books and wrote out the bills, and really they were both rather happy. Pridmore, disguised as the automatic machine, stood in the shop and attracted many customers. They used to bring their children, and make the poor innocents put their pennies in, and then read Pridmore's good advice. Some parents are so harsh. And the Princess sat in the back garden with the Cockatoucan, and Matilda played with her every afternoon. But one day, as the King was driving through another kingdom, the King of that kingdom looked out of one of his Palace windows, and laughed as the King went by, and shouted, "Butcher!"

The Butcher-King did not mind this, because it was true, however rude. But when the other King called out, "What price cat's meat!" the King was very angry indeed, because the meat he sold was always of the best quality. When he told Matilda all about it, she said, "Send the Army to crush him."

So the King sent his Army, and the enemy were crushed. The Bird laughed the King back into his throne, and laughed away the butcher's shop just in time for his Majesty to proclaim a general holiday, and to organise a magnificent reception for the Army. Matilda now helped the King to manage everything. She wonderfully enjoyed the new delightful feeling of being clever, so that she felt it was indeed too bad when the Cockatoucan laughed just as the reception was beautifully arranged. It laughed, and the general holiday was turned into an income tax; the magnificent reception changed itself to a royal reprimand, and the Army itself suddenly became a discontented Sunday-school treat, and

The king sent his army, and the enemy were crushed.

had to be fed with buns and brought home in brakes, crying.

"Something must be done," said the King.

"Well," said Matilda, "I've been thinking if you will make me the Princess's governess, I'll see what I can do. I'm quite clever enough."

"I must open Parliament to do that," said the King; "it's a Constitutional change."

So he hurried off down the road to open Parliament. But the bird put its head on one side and laughed at him as he went by. He hurried on, but his beautiful crown grew large and brassy, and was set with cheap glass in the worst possible taste. His robe turned from velvet and ermine to flannelette and rabbit's fur. His sceptre grew twenty feet long and extremely awk-

ward to carry. But he persevered, his
royal blood was up.

"No bird," said he, "shall keep me
from my duty and my Parliament."

But when he got there, he was so
agitated that he could not remember
which was the right key to open Parliament with, and in the end he hampered the lock and so could not open
Parliament at all, and members of Parliament went about making speeches
in the roads to the great hindrance of
the traffic.

The poor King went home and
burst into tears.

"Matilda," he said, "this is too
much. You have always been a comfort to me. You stood by me when I
was a butcher; you kept the books;
you booked the orders; you ordered
the stock. If you really are clever
enough, now is the time to help me.

If you won't, I'll give up the business. I'll leave off being a King. I'll go and be a butcher in the Camberwell New Road, and I will get another little girl to keep my books, not you."

This decided Matilda. She said, "Very well, your Majesty, then give me leave to prowl at night. Perhaps I shall find out what makes the Cocka-toucan laugh; if I can do that, we can take care he never gets it, whatever it is."

"Ah!" said the poor King, "if you could only do that."

When Matilda went to bed that night, she did not go to sleep. She lay and waited till all the Palace was quiet, and then she crept softly, pussily, mous-ily to the garden, where the Cocka-toucan's cage was, and she hid behind a white rosebush, and looked and lis-tened. Nothing happened till it was gray dawn, and then it was only the Cockatoucan who woke up. But when the sun was round and red over the Palace roof, something came creeping, creeping, pussily, mousily out of the Palace; and it looked like a yard and a half of white tape creeping along; and it was the Princess herself.

She came quietly up to the cage, and squeezed herself between the bars; they were very narrow bars, but a yard and a half of white tape can go through the bars of any birdcage I ever saw. And the Princess went up to the Cockatoucan and tickled him under his wings till he laughed aloud. Then, quick as thought, the Princess squeezed through the bars, and was back in her room before the bird had finished laughing. Matilda went back to bed. Next day all the sparrows had turned into cart horses, and the roads were impassable.

That day when she went, as usual, to play with the Princess, Matilda said to her suddenly, "Princess, what makes you so thin?"

The Princess caught Matilda's hand and pressed it with warmth.

"Matilda," she said simply, "you have a noble heart. No one else has ever asked me that, though they tried to cure it. And I couldn't answer till I was asked, could I? It's a sad, a tragic tale, Matilda. I was once as fat as you are."

"I'm not so very fat," said Matilda, indignantly.

"Well," said the Princess impatiently, "I was quite fat enough anyhow. And then I got thin—"

"But how?"

"Because they would not let me

have my favourite pudding every
day."

"What a shame!" said Matilda, "and
what is your favourite pudding?"

"Bread and milk, of course, sprin-
kled with rose leaves—and with pear-
drops in it."

Of course, Matilda went at once to
the King, and while she was on her
way the Cockatoucan happened to
laugh. When she reached the King, he
was in no condition for ordering dinner, for he had turned into a villa residence, replete with every modern im-
provement. Matilda only recognised
him, as he stood sadly in the Park, by
the crown that stuck crookedly on one
of the chimney-pots, and the border of
ermine along the garden path. So she
ordered the Princess's favourite pudding on her own responsibility, and
the whole Court had it every day for

The king had turned into a villa residence.

dinner, till there was no single courtier
but loathed the very sight of bread and
milk, and there was hardly one who
would not have run a mile rather than
meet a pear-drop. Even Matilda herself got rather tired of it, though being
clever, she knew how good bread and
milk was for her.

But the Princess got fatter and fatter,
and rosier and rosier. Her thread-paper
gowns had to be let out, and let out,
till there were no more turnings in left
to be let out, and then she had to wear
the old ones that Matilda had been
wearing, and then to have new ones.
And as she got fatter she got kinder, till
Matilda grew quite fond of her.

And the Cockatoucan had not
laughed for a month.

When the Princess was as fat as any
Princess ought to be, Matilda went to
her one day, and threw her arms

round her and kissed her. The Princess kissed her back, and said, "Very well, I *am* sorry then, but I didn't want to say so, but now I will. And the Cockatoucan never laughs except when he's tickled. So there! He hates to laugh."

"And you won't do it again," said Matilda, "will you?"

"No, of course not," said the Princess, very much surprised, "why should I? I was spiteful when I was thin, but now I'm fat again I want every one to be happy."

"But how can any one be happy?" asked Matilda, severely, "when every one is turned into something they weren't meant to be? There's your dear father—he's a desirable villa—the Prime Minister was a little boy, and he got back again, and now he's turned into a Comic Opera. Half the Palace housemaids are breakers, dashing themselves against the Palace crockery: the Navy, to a man, are changed to French poodles, and the Army to German sausages. Your favourite nurse is now a flourishing steam laundry, and I, alas! am too clever by half. Can't that horrible bird do anything to put us all right again?''

"No," said the Princess, dissolved in tears at this awful picture, "he told me once himself that when he laughed he could only change one or two things at once, and then, as often as not, it turned out to be something he didn't expect. The only way to make everything come right again would be—but it can't be done! If we could only make him laugh on the wrong side of his mouth. That's the secret. He told me so. But I don't know what it *is*, let alone being able to do it. Could *you* do it, Matilda?"

"No," said Matilda, "but let me whisper. He's listening. Pridmore could. She's often told me she'd do it to me. But she never has. Oh, Princess, I've got an idea."

The two were whispering so low that the Cockatoucan could not hear, though he tried his hardest. Matilda and the Princess left him listening.

Presently he heard a sound of wheels. Four men came into the rose-garden wheeling a great red thing in a barrow. They set it down in front of the Cockatoucan, who danced on his perch with rage.

"Oh," he said, "if only some one would make me laugh, that horrible thing would be the one to change. I know it would. It would change into something much horrider than it is now. I feel it in all my feathers."

The Princess opened the cage-door

*Four men came wheeling a great
red thing on a barrow.*

with the Prime Minister's key, which a tenor singer had found at the beginning of his music. It was also the key of the comic opera. She crept up behind the Cockatoucan and tickled him under both wings. He fixed his baleful eye on the red Automatic Machine and laughed long and loud; he saw the red iron and glass change before his eyes into the form of Pridmore. Her cheeks were red with rage and her eyes shone like glass with fury.

"Nice manners!" said she to the Cockatoucan, "what are you laughing at, I should like to know—I'll make you laugh on the wrong side of your mouth, my fine fellow!"

She sprang into the cage, and then and there, before the astonished Court, she shook that Cockatoucan till he really and truly did laugh on the wrong side of his mouth. It was a terrible sight to witness, and the sound of that wrong-sided laughter was horrible to hear.

But instantly all the things changed back as if by magic to what they had been before. The laundry became a nurse, the villa became a king, the other people were just what they had been before, and all Matilda's wonderful cleverness went out like the snuff of a candle.

The Cockatoucan himself fell in two—one half of him became a common, ordinary toucan, such as you must have seen a hundred times at the Zoo, unless you are unworthy to visit that happy place, and the other half became a weathercock, which, as you know, is always changing and makes the wind change too. So he has not quite lost his old power. Only now he is in halves, any power he may have has to be used without laughing. The poor, broken Cockatoucan, like King you-know-who in English history, has never since that sad day smiled again.

The grateful King sent an escort of the whole Army, now no longer dressed in sausage skins, but in uniforms of dazzling beauty, with drums and banners, to see Matilda and Pridmore home. But Matilda was very sleepy. She had been clever for so long that she was quite tired out. It is indeed a very fatiguing thing, as no doubt you know. And the soldiers must have been sleepy too, for one by one the whole Army disappeared, and by the time Pridmore and Matilda reached home there was only one left, and he was the policeman at the corner.

The next day Matilda began to talk to Pridmore about the Green Land

and the Cockatoucan and the Villa-residence-King, but Pridmore only said—

"Pack of nonsense! Hold your tongue, do!"

So Matilda naturally understood that Pridmore did not wish to be reminded of the time when she was an Automatic Nagging Machine, so of course, like a kind and polite little girl, she let the subject drop.

Matilda did not mention her adventures to the others at home because she saw that they believed her to have spent the time with her Great-aunt Willoughby.

And she knew if she had said that she had not been there she would be sent at once—and she did not wish this.

She has often tried to get Pridmore to take the wrong omnibus again, which is the only way she knows of getting to the Green Land; but only once has she been successful, and then the omnibus did not go to the Green Land at all, but to the Elephant and Castle.

But no little girl ought to expect to go to the Green Land more than once in a lifetime. Many of us indeed are not even so fortunate as to go there once.

Whereyouwantogoto

OR THE BOUNCIBLE BALL

I T is very hard, when you have been accustomed to go to the seaside every summer ever since you were quite little, to be made to stay in London just because an aunt and an uncle choose to want to come and stay at your house to see the Royal Academy and go to the summer sales.

Selim and Thomasina felt that it was very hard indeed. And aunt and uncle were not the nice kind, either. If it had been Aunt Emma, who dressed dolls and told fairy-tales—or Uncle Reggie, who took you to the Crystal Palace, and gave you five bob at a time, and never even asked what you spent it on, it would have been different. But it was Uncle Thomas and Aunt Selina.

Aunt Selina was all beady, and sat bolt upright, and told you to mind what you were told, and Selim had been named after her—as near as they could get. And Uncle Thomas was the one Thomasina had been named after: he was deaf, and he always told you what the moral of everything was, and the housemaid said he was "near."

"I know he is, worse luck," said Thomasina.

"I mean, miss," explained the housemaid, "he's none too free with his chink."

Selim groaned. "He never gave me but a shilling in his life," said he, "and that turned out to be bad when I tried to change it at the ginger-beer shop."

The children could not understand why this aunt and uncle were allowed to interfere with everything as they did: and they quite made up their minds that when they were grown up they would never allow an aunt or an uncle to cross their doorsteps. They never thought—poor, dear little things—that some day they would grow up to be aunts and uncles in their turn, or, at least, one of each.

It was very hot in London that year: the pavement was like hot pie, and the asphalt was like hot pudding, and there was a curious wind that collected dust and straw and dirty paper, and then got tired of its collection, and threw it away in respectable people's areas and front gardens. The blind in the nursery had never been fixed up since the day when the children took it down to make a drop-scene for a play they were going to write and never did. So the hot afternoon sun came burning in through the window, and the children got hotter and hotter, and crosser and crosser, till at last Selim slapped Thomasina's arms till she cried, and Thomasina kicked Selim's legs till he screamed.

Then they sat down in different corners of the nursery and cried, and called each other names, and said they wished they were dead. This is very naughty indeed, as, of course, you know; but you must remember how hot it was.

When they had called each other all the names they could think of Thomasina said, suddenly, "All right, Silly," (that was Selim's pet name)— "cheer up."

"It's too hot to cheer up," said Selim, gloomily.

"We've been very naughty," said Thomasina, rubbing her eyes with the paint rag, "but it's all the heat. I heard Aunt Selina telling mother the weather wore her nerves to fiddle-strings. That just meant she was cross."

"Then it's not *our* fault," said Selim. "People say be good and you'll be happy. Uncle Reggy says, 'Be happy, and perhaps you'll be good.' *I* could be good if I was happy."

"So could I," said Thomasina.

"What *would* make you happy?" said a thick, wheezy voice from the toy cupboard, and out rolled the big green and red india-rubber ball that Aunt Emma had sent them last week. They had not played with it much, because the garden was so hot and sunny—and when they wanted to play with it in the street, on the shady side, Aunt Selina had said it was not like respectable children, so they weren't allowed.

Now the Ball rolled out very slowly—and the bright light on its new paint seemed to make it wink at them. You will think that they were surprised to hear a ball speak. Not at all. As you grow up, and more and more strange things happen to you, you will find that the more astonishing a thing is the less it surprises you. (I wonder why this is. Think it over, and write and tell me what you think.)

Selim stood up, and said, "Halloa"; but that was only out of politeness. Thomasina answered the Ball's question.

"We want to be at the seaside—and no aunts—and none of the things we don't like—and no uncles, of course," she said.

"Well," said the Ball, "if you think you can be good, why not set me bouncing?"

"We're not allowed in here," said Thomasina, "because of the crinkly ornaments people give me on my birthdays."

"Well, the street then," said the Ball; "the nice shady side."

"It's not like respectable children," said Selim sadly.

The Ball laughed. If you have never heard an india-rubber ball laugh you won't understand. It's the sort of quicker, quicker, quicker, softer, softer, softer chuckle of a bounce that it gives when it's settling down when you're tired of bouncing it.

"The garden, then," it said.

"I don't mind, if you'll go on talking," said Selim kindly.

So they took the Ball down into the garden and began to bounce it in the sun, on the dry, yellowy grass of the lawn.

"Come on," said the Ball. "You do like me!"

"What?" said the children.

"Why, do like I do—bounce!" said the Ball. "That's right—higher, higher, higher!"

For then and there the two children had begun bouncing as if their feet were india-rubber balls, and you have no idea what a delicious sensation that gives you.

"Higher, higher," cried the green and red ball, bouncing excitedly. "Now, follow me, higher, higher." And off it bounced down the blackened gravel of the path, and the children bounced after it, shrieking with delight at the new feeling. They bounced over the wall—all three of them—and the children looked back just in time to see Uncle Thomas tapping at the window, and saying, "Don't."

You have not the least idea how glorious it is to feel full of bouncibleness; so that, instead of dragging one foot after the other, as you do when you feel tired or naughty, you bounce along, and every time your feet touch the ground you bounce higher, and all without taking any trouble or tiring yourself. You have, perhaps, heard of the Greek gentleman who got new strength every time he fell down. His name was Antæus, and I believe he was an india-rubber ball, green on one side where he touched the earth, and red on the other where he felt the sun. But enough of classical research.

Thomasina and Selim bounced away, following the Bouncible Ball. They went over fences and walls, and through parched, dry gardens and burning-hot streets; they passed the region where fields of cabbages and rows of yellow brick cottages mark the division between London and the suburbs. They bounced through the suburbs, dusty and neat, with geraniums in the front gardens, and all the blinds pulled half-way down; and then the lamp-posts in the road got fewer and fewer, and the fields got greener and the hedges thicker—it was real, true country—with lanes instead of roads; and down the lanes the green and red Ball went bouncing, bouncing, bouncing, and the children after it. Thomasina, in her white, starched

They bounced through the suburbs.

frock, very prickly round the neck, and Selim, in his every-day sailor-suit, a little tight under the arms. His Sunday one was a size larger. No one seemed to notice them, but they noticed and pitied the children who were being "taken for a walk" in the gritty suburban roads.

"Where are we going?" they asked the Ball, and it answered, with a sparkling green and red smile—

"To the most delightful place in the world."

"What's it called?" asked Selim.

"It's called Whereyouwantogoto," the Ball answered, and on they went. It was a wonderful journey—up and down, looking through the hedges and over them, looking in at the doors of cottages, and then in at the top windows, up and down—bounce—bounce—bounce.

And at last they came to the sea. And the Bouncing Ball said, "Here you are! Now be good, for there's nothing here but the things that make people happy." And with that he curled himself up like a ball in the shadow of a wet sea-weedy rock, and went to sleep, for he was tired out with his long journey. The children stopped bouncing, and looked about them.

"Oh, Tommy;" said Selim.

"Oh, Silly!" said Thomasina. And well they might! In the place to which the Ball had brought them was all that your fancy can possibly paint, and a great deal more beside.

The children feel exactly as you do when you've had the long, hot, dirty train journey—and every one has been so cross about the boxes and the little brown portmanteau that was left be-

hind at the junction—and then when
you get to your lodgings you are told
that you may run down and have a
look at the sea if you're back by tea
time, and mother and nurse will un-
pack.

Only Thomasina and her brother
had not had a tiresome journey—and
there were no nasty, stuffy lodgings for
them, and no tea with oil butter and a
new pot of marmalade.

"There's silver-sand," said she—
"miles of it."

"And rocks," said he.

"And cliffs."

"And caves in the cliffs."

"And how cool it is," said Thomasina.

"And yet it's nice and warm too,"
said Selim.

"And what shells!"

"And seaweed."

"And the downs behind!"

"And trees in the distance!"

"And here's a dog, to go after sticks. Here, Rover, Rover."

A big black dog answered at once to the name, because he was a retriever, and they are all called Rover.

"And spades!" said the girl.

"And pails!" said the boy.

"And what pretty sea-poppies," said the girl.

"And a basket—and grub in it!" said the boy. So they sat down and had lunch.

It was a lovely lunch. Lobsters and ice-creams (strawberry and pine-apple), and toffee and hot buttered toast and ginger-beer. They ate and ate, and thought of the aunt and uncle at home, and the minced veal and sago pudding, and they were very happy indeed.

The seal was very kind and convenient.

Just as they were finishing their lunch they saw a swirling, swishing, splashing commotion in the green sea a little way off, and they tore off their clothes and rushed into the water to see what it was. It was a seal. He was very kind and convenient. He showed them how to swim and dive.

"But won't it make us ill to bathe so soon after meals? Isn't it wrong?" asked Thomasina.

"Not at all," said the seal. "Nothing is wrong here—as long as you're good. Let me teach you water-leap-frog—a most glorious game, so cool, yet so exciting. You try it."

At last the seal said: "I suppose you wear man-clothes. They're very inconvenient. My two eldest have just outgrown their coats. If you'll accept them—"

And it dived, and came up with two

golden sealskin coats over its arm, and the children put them on.

"Thank you very much," they said. "You *are* kind."

I am almost sure that it has never been your luck to wear a fur coat that fitted you like a skin, and that could not be spoiled with sand or water, or jam, or bread and milk, or any of the things with which you mess up the nice new clothes your kind relations buy for you. But if you like, you may try to imagine how jolly the little coats were.

Thomasina and Selim played all day on the beach, and when they were tired they went into a cave, and found supper—salmon and cucumber, and welsh-rabbit and lemonade—and then they went to bed in a great heap of straw and grass and fern and dead leaves, and all the delightful things you have often wished to sleep in. Only you have never been allowed to.

In the morning there were plum-pudding for breakfast, and roast duck and lemon jelly, and the day passed like a happy dream, only broken by surprising and delightful meals. The Ball woke up and showed them how to play water-polo; and they bounced him on the sand, with shrieks of joy and pleasure. You know, a Ball likes to be bounced by people he is fond of— it is like slapping a friend on the shoulder.

There were no houses in "Where-youwantogoto," and no bathing machines or bands, no nursemaids or policemen or aunts or uncles. You could do exactly what you liked as long as you were good.

"What will happen if we are

naughty?" Selim asked. The Ball looked very grave, and answered—

"I must not tell you; and I very strongly advise you not to try to find out."

"We won't—indeed, we won't," said they, and went off to play rounders with the rabbits on the downs— who were friendly fellows, and very keen on the game.

On the third evening Thomasina was rather silent, and the Ball said, "What's the matter, girl-bouncer? Out with it."

So she said, "I was wondering how mother is, and whether she has one of her bad headaches."

The Ball said, "Good little girl! Come with me and I'll show you something."

He bounced away, and they followed him, and he flopped into a rocky pool, frightening the limpets and sea-anemones dreadfully, though he did not mean to.

"Now look," he called from under the water, and the children looked, and the pool was like a looking-glass, only it was not their own faces they saw in it.

They saw the drawing-room at home, and father and mother, who were both quite well, only they looked tired—and the aunt and uncle were there—and Uncle Thomas was saying, "What a blessing those children are away."

"Then they know where we are?" said Selim to the Ball.

"They think they know," said the Ball, "or you think they think they know. Anyway, they're happy enough. Good-night."

And he curled himself up like a ball

in his favourite sleeping-place. The two children crept into their pleasant, soft, sweet nest of straw and leaves and fern and grass, and went to sleep. But Selim was vexed with Thomasina because she had thought of mother before he had, and he said she had taken all the fern—and they went to sleep rather cross. They woke crosser. So far they had both helped to make the bed every morning, but to-day neither wanted to.

"I don't see why I should make the beds," said he; "it's a girl's work, not a boy's."

"I don't see why I should do it," said Thomasina; "it's a servant's place, not a young lady's."

And then a very strange and terrible thing happened. Quite suddenly, out of nothing and out of nowhere, ap-

peared a housemaid—large and stern
and very neat indeed, and she said—

"You are quite right, miss; it is my
place to make the beds. And I am in-
structed to see that you are both in
bed by seven."

Think how dreadful this must have
been to children who had been going
to bed just when they felt inclined.
They went out on to the beach.

"You see what comes of being
naughty," said Thomasina; and Selim
said, "Oh, shut up, do!"

They cheered up towards dinner-
time—it was roast pigeons that day
and bread sauce, and whitebait and
syllabubs—and for the rest of the day
they were as good as gold, and very
polite to the Ball. Selim told it all
about the dreadful apparition of the
housemaid, and it shook its head (I
know *you've* never seen a ball do that,

*Suddenly, out of nothing and nowhere,
appeared a large, stern housemaid.*

and very likely you never will) and said—

"My Bouncible Boy, you may be happy here for ever and ever if you're contented and good. Otherwise— well, it's a quarter to seven—you've got to go."

And, sure enough they had to. And the housemaid put them to bed, and washed them with yellow soap, and some of it got in their eyes. And she lit a night-light, and sat with them till they went to sleep, so that they couldn't talk, and were ever so much longer getting to sleep than they would have been if she had not been there. And the beds were iron, with mattresses and hot, stuffy, fluffy sheets and many more new blankets than they wanted.

The next day they got out as early as they could and played water football with the seal and the Bouncible Ball, and when dinner-time came it was lobster and ices. But Thomasina was in a bad temper. She said, "I wish it was duck." And before the words had left her lips it was cold mutton and rice-pudding, and they had to sit up to table and eat it properly too, and the housemaid came round to see that they didn't leave any bits on the edges of their plates, or talk with their mouths full.

There were no more really nice meals after that, only the sort of things you get at home. But is is possible to be happy even without really nice meals. But you have to be very careful. The days went by pleasantly enough. All the sea and land creatures were most kind and attentive. The seal taught them all it knew, and was always ready to play with them. The star-fish taught them astronomy, and the jelly-fish taught them fancy cooking. The limpets taught them dancing as well as they could for their lameness. The sea-birds taught them to make nests—a knowledge they have never needed to apply—and if the oysters did not teach them anything it was only because oysters are so very stupid, and not from any lack of friendly feeling.

The children bathed every day in the sea, and if they had only been content with this all would have been well. But they weren't.

"Let's dig a bath," said Selim, "and the sea will come in and fill it, and then we can bathe in it."

So they fetched their spades and dug—and there was no harm in that, as you very properly remark.

But when the hole was finished,

and the sea came creep, creep, creep-ing up—and at last a big wave thun-dered up the sand and swirled into the hole, Thomasina and Selim were struggling on the edge, fighting which should go in first, and the wave drew sandily back into the sea, and neither of them had bathed in the new bath. And now it was all wet and sandy, and its nice sharp edges rounded off, and much shallower. And as they looked at it angrily, the sandy bottom of the bath stirred and shifted and rose up, as if some great sea-beast were heaving un-derneath with his broad back. The wet sand slipped back in slabs at each side, and a long pointed thing like a thin cow's back came slowly up. It showed broader and broader, and presently the flakes of wet sand were dropping heavily off the top of a brand-new bathing machine that stood on the sand over where their bath had been.

"Well," said Selim, "we've done it this time."

They certainly had, for on the door of the bathing machine was painted: "You must not bathe any more except through me."

So there was no more running into the sea just when and how they liked. They had to use the bathing machine, and it smelt of stale salt water and other people's wet towels.

After this the children did not seem to care so much about the seaside, and they played more on the downs, where the rabbits were very kind and hospitable, and in the woods, where all sorts of beautiful flowers grew wild—and there was nobody to say "Don't" when you picked them. The children thought of what Uncle

YOU MUST NOT BATHE ANY MORE EXCEPT THROUGH ME!

A long, pointed thing came slowly up out of the sand.

Thomas would have said if he had been there, and they were very, very happy.

But one day Thomasina had pulled a lot of white convolvulus and some pink geraniums and calceolarias—the kind you are never allowed to pick at home—and she had made a wreath of them and put it on her head.

Then Selim said. "You *are* silly! You look like a Bank Holiday."

And his sister said, "I can't help it. They'd look lovely on a hat, if they were only artificial. I wish I had a hat."

And she had. A large stiff hat that hurt her head just where the elastic was sewn on, and she had her stiff white frock that scratched, her tiresome underclothing, all of it, and stockings and heavy boots; and Selim had his sailor suit—the every-day one that was too tight in the arms; and they had to wear them always, and their fur coats were taken away.

They went sadly, all stiff and uncomfortable, and told the Bouncible Ball. It looked very grave, and great tears of salt water rolled down its red and green cheeks as it sat by the wet, seaweed-covered rock.

"Oh, you silly children," it said, "haven't you been warned enough? You've everything a reasonable child could wish for. Can't you be contented?"

"Of course we can," they said—and so they were—for a day and a half. And then it wasn't exactly discontent but real naughtiness that brought them to grief.

They were playing on the downs by the edge of the wood under the heliotrope tree. A hedge of camellia bushes cast a pleasant shadow, and out in the open sunlight on the downs the orchids grew like daisies, and the carnations like buttercups. All about was that kind of turf on which the gardener does not like you to play, and they had pulled armfuls of lemon verbena and made a bed of it. But Selim's blouse was tight under the arms. So when Thomasina said—

"Oh, Silly dear, how beautiful it is, just like fairyland," he said—

"Silly yourself. There's no such thing as fairyland."

Just then a fairy, with little bright wings the colour of a peacock's tail, fluttered across the path, and settled on a magnolia flower.

"Oh! Silly darling," cried Thomasina, "it *is* fairyland, and there's a fairy, such a beautiful dear. Look—there she goes."

But Selim would not look—he turned over and hid his eyes.

"There's no such thing as fairyland, I tell you," he grunted, "and I don't believe in fairies."

And then, quite suddenly and very horribly the fairy turned into a policeman—because every one knows there are such things as policemen, and any one can believe in *them*.

And all the rare and beautiful flowers withered up and disappeared, and only thorns and thistles were left, and the misty, twiny trim little grass path that led along the top of the cliffs turned into a parade, and the policeman walked up and down it incessantly, and watched the children at their play, and you know how difficult it is to play when any one is watching you, especially a policeman. Selim was extremely vexed: that was why, he

It is difficult to play when any one is watching
you, especially a policeman.

said, there couldn't possibly be glow-worms as big as bicycle lamps, which, of course, there were in "Whereyou-wantogoto." It was after that that the gas-lamps were put all along the parade, and a pier sprang up on purpose to be lighted with electricity, and a band played, because it is nonsense to have a pier without a band.

"Oh, you naughty, silly children," said the Bouncible Ball, turning red with anger, except in the part where he was green with disgust; "it makes me bounce with rage to see how you've thrown away your chances, and what a seaside resort you're making of 'Whereyouwantogoto.' "

And he did bounce, angrily, up and down the beach till the housemaid looked out of the cave and told the children not to be so noisy, and the policeman called out—

"Now then, move along there, move along. You're obstructing of the traffic."

And now I have something to tell you which you will find it hard to make any excuses for. I can't make any myself. I can only ask you to remember how hard it is to be even moderately good, and how easy it is to be extremely naughty.

When the Bouncible Ball stopped bouncing, Selim said—

"I wonder what makes him bounce."

"Oh no, *don't!*" cried Thomasina, for she had heard her brother wonder that about balls before, and she knew all too well what it ended in.

"Oh, *don't,*" she said, "oh, Silly, he brought us here, he's been so kind." But Selim said, "Nonsense; balls can't feel, and it will be almost as good to play with after I've looked inside it."

And then, before Thomasina could prevent him, he pulled out the knife Uncle Reggy gave him last holiday but one, and catching the Ball up, he plunged the knife into its side. The Bouncible Ball uttered one whiffing squeak of pain and grief, then with a low, hissing sigh its kindly spirit fled, and it lay, a lifeless mass of paint and india-rubber in the hands of its assassin. Thomasina burst into tears—but the heartless Selim tore open the Ball, and looked inside. You know well enough what he found there. Emptiness; the little square patch of india-rubber that makes the hard lump on the outside of the ball which you feel with your fingers when the ball is alive and his own happy, bouncing, cheerful self.

The children stood looking at each other.

"I—I almost wish I hadn't," said Selim at last; but before Thomasina could answer he had caught her hand.

"Oh, look," he cried, "look at the sea."

It was, indeed, a dreadful sight. The beautiful dancing, sparkling blue sea was drying up before their eyes—in less than a moment it was quite flat and dusty. It hurriedly laid down a couple of railway lines, and up a signal-box and telegraph-poles, and became the railway at the back of their house at home.

The children, gasping with horror, turned to the downs. From them tall, yellow brick houses were rising, as if drawn up by an invisible hand. Just as treacle does in cold weather if you put your five fingers in and pulled them

up. But, of course, you are never allowed to do this. The beach got
hard—it was a pavement. The green
downs turned grey—they were slate
roofs—and Thomasina and Selim
found themselves at the iron gate of
their own number in the terrace—and
there was Uncle Thomas at the window knocking for them to come in,
and Aunt Selina calling out to them
how far from respectable it was to play
in the streets.

They were sent to bed at once—
that was Aunt Selina's suggestion—
and Uncle Thomas arranged that they
should have only dry bread for tea.

Selim and Thomasina have never
seen "Whereyouwantogoto" again,
nor the Bouncible Ball—not even his
poor body—and they don't deserve to
either. Of course, Thomasina was not
so much to blame as Selim, but she

was punished just the same. I can't help that. This is really the worst of being naughty. You not only have to suffer for it yourself, but some one else always has to suffer too, generally the person who loves you best.

You are intelligent children, and I will not insult you with a moral. I am not Uncle Thomas. Nor will I ask you to remember what I have told you. I am not Aunt Selina.

The Prince, Two Mice, and Some Kitchen-Maids

WHEN the Prince was born the Queen said to the King, "My dear, do be very, very careful about the invitations. You know what fairies are. They always come to the christening whether you invite them or not, and if you forget to invite one of them she always makes herself so terribly unpleasant."

"My love," said the King, "I will invite them all," and he took out his diamond-pointed pen and wrote out the cards on the spot.

But just then a herald came in to bring news of war. So the King had to go off in a hurry. The invitations were sent out, but the christening had to be put off for a year. At the end of this time the King had subdued all his enemies, so he was very pleased with himself. The Prince was a year old, and he also was pleased with himself, as all good babies are, and found the little royal fingers and toes a fresh and ever-delightful mystery. And the Queen was pleased with herself, as all good mothers should be—so everything went merrily. The Palace was hung with cloth of silver and strewn with fresh daisies, in honour of the great day, and after all had eaten and drunk to their hearts' content the fairies came near with the gifts they had brought to their godson the Prince.

"He shall have beauty," said the first.

"And wit," said the second.

"And a pretty sweetheart," said the third; "who loves him," said the fourth.

And so they went on, foretelling for him all sorts of happy and desirable things. And as each fairy gave her gift she stooped and kissed the baby Prince, and then spreading her fine gossamer-gauze wings, fluttered away across the rosy garden. The crowd of fairies grew less and less, and there were only three left when the Queen pulled the King's sleeve and whispered, "My dear, where's Malevola?"

"I sent her a card," said the King, casting an anxious look round him.

"Then it must have been lost on the way," said the Queen, "or she'd have been here—"

"She *is* here," said a low voice in the Queen's ear. Suddenly the room grew dark, grey clouds hid the sun, and all the daisies on the floor shut up quite close. The poor Queen gave a start and a scream, and the King, brave as he was, turned pale, for Malevola was a terrible fairy, and the dress she wore was not at all the thing for a christening. It was made of spiders' webs matted together, dark and dank with the damp of the tomb and the dust of dungeons. Her wings were the wings of a great bat; spiders and newts crawled round her neck; a serpent coiled about her waist and little snakes twisted and writhed in her straight black hair.

She looked at the Queen so terribly that her poor Mother-Majesty cried out without meaning to.

"Oh don't!" she cried, and flung

*Malevola's dress was not at all
the thing for a christening.*

both arms round the cradle. The Prince was quite happy, playing with his new coral and bells, and looking at the Palace cat, who sat at the foot of the cradle washing herself.

"Now listen," said Malevola, still speaking in the low, even voice that was so terrible. "You did not invite me to the christening. I've read my fairy tales, and I know what's expected of a fairy who is left out on an occasion like this. I intend to curse your son."

Then all the Kings and Queens who had come to the christening wished they had stayed away, and they and all the Court fell on their knees and begged Malevola for mercy. As for the three good fairies who were left, they hid behind the window-curtains, and the Court ladies, peeping between their fingers, said—

"Fancy deserting their godson like this! How unfairy-like!"

But the Queen and the King only wept, and the Prince played with his rattle and looked at the cat.

Then Malevola said mockingly: "Great King and mighty Sovereign, Malevola was not good enough to be asked to your tea-party. But your family shall come down in the world; your son shall marry a kitchen-maid and marry a lady with four feet and no hands."

A shiver of horror ran through the room, and Malevola vanished. Then, suddenly, the sun came out, and people lifted up their heads, and dared again to look at each other. And the daisies, too, opened their eyes again.

Then the good fairies came out from behind the window-curtains, and the poor Queen fell on her knees before them.

"Can't you do *anything*?" she asked. "Can't you undo what she says, and make it untrue?"

"Not even a fairy can make a true thing untrue," said the good fairies sadly. "Malevola's words will come true; but the Prince has already many gifts, and our gifts are yet to give, and these you shall choose. Whatever you wish shall be his."

Then the King, recovering a little from the terror into which the fairy Malevola had thrown him, and remembering how well he and his royal line had always borne them in battle, said at once—

"Let the boy be brave."

"He is brave," said one of the good fairies; "he fears nothing."

And at this the Prince ceased to feel

any fear of the Palace cat. He put out
his hand and pulled her tail so merrily
that Pussy turned and clawed the little
arm till the blood ran.

"Oh, dear!" cried his mother, "he is
fearless, as you say. I wish he were
afraid of cats, poor darling."

"He is," said the second fairy; "you
have your wish." And, indeed, the
Prince screamed, and hid his face, and
shrank from the Palace cat with such
horror that the King pulled out his
pencil and note-book and wrote an
edict then and there banishing all cats
from his dominions. But, all the same,
he was very angry.

"Your Majesty has wasted one
wish," he said very politely to the
Queen; "let us now leave the last gift
in the hands of the last fairy."

The last fairy came and kissed the
Prince, who was now sobbing sleepily.

"He shall be happy," she said; "he shall have his heart's desire."

Then she too vanished; and the Kings and Queens took their leave when their gold coaches came for them. And presently the King and Queen were left alone with the silver hangings and the strewn daisies and the baby.

"Oh dear! oh dear!" said the Queen; "this is dreadful! A kitchen-maid!—and a lady with four feet and no hands!"

"At least we are not likely to have a kitchen-maid with less than two hands," said the King.

"We might arrange only to have *ti-tled* kitchen-maids," said the Queen timidly.

"The very thing," the King answered: "that would make the love affair all that one could wish. But there's still the marriage."

"Of course he'll marry the lady he loves."

"It's not the way of the world," said the King. "At any rate, let's hope he'll love the lady he marries. Otherwise—"

"Otherwise what?" said the Queen.

"We know nothing about otherwise, do we, my Queen?" he said, catching her round the waist. And in his love for his wife and his son the King felt almost happy again, for here they were all three together, and when your son is in his cradle his marriage seems very far off indeed.

But the Queen was anxious and frightened, and while the Prince was still a child she sent messengers to the Courts of all the neighbouring Kings and Queens to tell them what had been foretold, which, indeed, most of them knew, having been at the christening. And she begged such of them as had daughters to send them as kitchen-maids, that so the Prince might at least fall in love with a real Princess. And as the Prince grew up he was so handsome and so brave, fearing nothing but cats, which, of course, he never saw, though he dreamed of them often and woke screaming, and also so brilliant and good, that, his father's kingdom, being beyond compare the finest in all the round world, the young daughters of Kings vied with each other as to who should find favour in the eyes of the Queen-Mother, and so get leave to serve in the kitchen, each nursing the hope that some day the Prince would see her and love her, and perhaps even marry her. And he was very good friends with all the noble kitchen-maids, but he loved none of them, till one day he saw, at a window of the tower where the kitchen was, a bright face and bright hair tied round with a scarlet kerchief. And as he looked at the face it was withdrawn—but the Prince had lost his heart. He kept his secret safe in the place where his heart had been, and schemed and plotted to see this fair lady again; for when he went among the royal kitchen-maids she was not there with them. And he looked morning, noon, and evening, but he never could see her. So then he said—

"I must watch o' nights—perhaps she is kept in prison in the tower above the kitchen, and at night those who watch her may sleep, and so I shall be able to talk to her."

So he dressed in dark clothes and

hid in the shadow of the palace courtyard and watched all one night. And
he saw nothing. But in the early
morning, when the setting moon and
the rising sun were mixing their lights
in the sky, he heard a heavy bolt shot
back, and the door of the kitchen
tower opened slowly. The Prince
crouched behind a buttress and
watched, and he saw the fair maid
with the bright hair under the red kerchief. She swept the doorstep, and she
drew water from the well in the middle of the courtyard; and presently he
crept to the kitchen window and saw
her light the fire and wash the dishes,
and make all neat and clean within.
And the Prince's eyes followed her in
all she did, and the more he looked at
her the more he loved her. And at last
he heard sounds as of folks stirring
above, so he crept away, keeping close

to the wall, and so back to his own rooms. And this he did again on the next morning, and on the next. And on the third morning, as he stood looking through the window at the girl with the bright hair and the bright kerchief, the gold chain he wore clinked against the stone of the window-sill. The maid started, and the bowl she held dropped on to the brick floor of the kitchen and broke into twenty pieces; and then and there she sat down on the floor beside it, and began to cry bitterly.

The Prince ran in and knelt beside her.

"Don't cry, dear," he said, "I'll get you another bowl."

"It isn't that," she sobbed, "but now they'll send me away."

"Who will?"

"The noble Kitchen-Maids. They

keep me to do the work because, being Kings' daughters, they don't know how to do anything; but the Queen doesn't know that there is a Real Kitchen-maid here, and now you have found out they will send me away."

And she went on crying.

"Then you are a Real Kitchen-maid, and not noble at all?" said the Prince.

She stopped crying for a minute to say "No."

"Never mind," said the Prince. "You are twice as pretty as all the Kings' daughters put together and twenty times as dear."

At that she stopped crying for good and all, and looked up at him from the floor where she sat.

"Yes you are," he said, "and I love you with all my heart."

And with that he caught her in his

arms and kissed her; and the Real Kitchen-Maid laid her face against his, and her heart beat wildly, for she knew what the Prince did not, and what, indeed, all the folk knew except the Prince, that this had been foretold at his christening; but she knew also that though he loved her, he was not to marry her, since it was his dreadful destiny to marry some one with four feet and no hands.

"I wish I had no hands and four feet," said the Real Kitchen-maid to herself. "I wouldn't mind a bit, since it is me he loves."

"What are you saying?" asked the Prince.

"I am saying that you must go," said she. "If their Kitchen Highnesses find you here with me they'll tear me into little pieces, for they all love you—to a Highness."

"And you," he whispered, "how much do you love me?"

"Oh," she answered, "I love you better than my right hand and my left."

And the Prince thought that a very strange answer. He went through that day in a happy dream; but he did not tell his dream to any one, lest some harm should come to the Real Kitchen-Maid. For he meant to marry her, and he had a feeling that his parents would not approve of the match.

Now that night, when the whole palace was asleep, the Real Kitchen-Maid got up and crept out past the sleepy sentinel and went home to her father the farmer and got one of his great white cart horses and rode away through the woods to the cavern where the Great White Rat sits sleeplessly guarding the Magic Cat's-eye.

And every one wondered why he guarded it so carefully, for it seemed to have no great value. But the Great White Rat watched it constantly, without ever closing one of those round bright rat'-eyes of his, and when folk sought to lay hands on it he said—

"Be careful: it has the power to change you into a mouse."

On which folk dropped it hastily and went their ways, leaving him still on guard.

To him now went the little Kitchen-Maid, and asked for help, for he was thousands of years old, and had more wisdom between his nose and ears than all the books in all the world. She told him all that had happened.

"Now what shall I do?" she said. And the Great White Rat, never shifting his eyes from the Magic Cat's-eye, answered—

"Keep your own counsel and be contented. The Prince loves you."

"But," said the Real Kitchen-Maid, "he is not to marry me, but a horrible creature with four feet and no hands."

"Keep your secret and be content," the Great White Rat repeated, "and if ever you see him in danger from a lady with four feet and no hands, come straight to me."

So the Real Kitchen-Maid went back to the Palace, and set to work to clean pots and pans, for now it was bright dewy daylight, and the night had gone. And before the rest were awake again her Prince came to her and vowed he loved her more than life; so she kept her secret and was content.

At the time of the Prince's christen-

ing the King had banished all cats from
the kingdom, because he could not
bear to see his son show fear of anything. But now and then strangers, not
knowing of the edict, brought cats to
that country, and if the Prince saw one
of these cats he was taken with a trembling and a paleness, standing like
stone awhile, and presently, with
shrieks of terror, fleeing the spot. And
it was now a long time since he had
seen a cat.

Now, soon after the Prince had
found out how he loved the Real
Kitchen-Maid, his father and mother
died suddenly as they were sitting
hand in hand, for they loved each
other so much that it was not possible
for either to stay here without the
other.

So then the Prince wept bitterly,
and would not be comforted, and the

Court stood about him with a long face, wearing its new mourning. And as he sat there with his face hidden Something came through the Palace gate and up the marble stairs and into the great hall where the Prince sat on the steps of his father's throne weeping. And, before the courtiers could draw breath or decide whether it was Court etiquette for them to do anything while the Prince was crying except to stand still and look sad, the creature came up to the Prince and began to rub itself against his arm. And he, still hiding his face, reached out his hand and stroked it!

Then all the Court drew a deep breath, for they saw that the thing that had come in was a great black Cat.

And the Prince raised his eyes, and they looked to see him shrink and shriek; but instead he passed his hand over the black fur and said—

"Poor Pussy, then!"

And at these words the whole Court fled—by window and door. The courtiers took horse, those who had carriages went away in them, those who had none went on foot, and in less than a minute the Prince and the Cat were left alone together.

For the Court was learned in witch law, and knowing the Prince's horror of cats it saw at once that a cat he was not afraid of was no cat at all, but a witch in that shape. Therefore the courtiers and the whole Royal household fled trembling and hid themselves.

All but the little Real Kitchen-Maid. She saw with terror that the Cat, or rather the witch in Cat's shape, had done what no one else could do— roused the Prince from his dull dream of grief. And then she remembered the fate which Malevola had foretold for him—that he should marry a lady with four feet and no hands.

"Alack-a-day!" she cried. "This witch has four feet and no hands; but she can have hands whenever she chooses, and be a woman by her magic arts as easily as she can be a cat. And then he will love her—and what will become of me? Or, worse, she may marry him only to torment him. She may shut him up in some enchanted dungeon far from the light of day. Such things have happened before now."

So she stood, hidden by the blue arras, and wrung her hands, and the tears ran down her cheeks. And all the time the black Cat purred to the Prince, and the Prince stroked the black Cat, and any one could have seen that he was every moment becoming more deeply bewitched. And still the Real Kitchen-Maid crouched behind the arras, and her heart ached that it knew no way to save him. Then suddenly she remembered the words of the Great White Rat—

"If ever you see him in danger from a lady with four feet and no hands come straight to me."

Now surely was the time, for the Prince, she knew, was in desperate danger.

The Real Kitchen-Maid crept silently down the marble stairs, but once she was out of the Palace she ran like the wind to the stable. No men were about there—all had followed the example of the Court, and had run away when they heard of the strange coming of the witch-Cat. And of all the many horses that had stood in the stable only one remained, for each man

in his fright had saddled the first horse
that came to hand and ridden off on it.
And the one that still stayed there was
the Prince's own black charger. He
had had no mind to be saddled in haste
by a stranger, and had turned and bit-
ten the stranger who had attempted it.
So he was there alone.

Now the little Kitchen-Maid lifted
the Prince's gold-broidered saddle
from its perch, and the weight of it
was such that she could not have carried it but for the heavy heart she bore
because of her love to the Prince and
his danger, and that made all else seem
light. She put the saddle on the
charger, and the jewelled bridle. And
he nieghed with pleasure, for he understood, being a horse who could see
as far into a stone wall as most people.
And when he was saddled he knelt for
her to mount, and then up and away

like the wind, and she had no need to guide him with the reins, for he found the way and kept it. He galloped steadily on, and the sun went down and the night drew dark, and he went on, and on, and on without stumble or pause, till at moonrise he halted before the house of the Great White Rat.

Then, as the Real Kitchen-Maid sprang down, the Great White Rat came out from his house and spoke. "You've come for it, then?"

"For what?"

"The Magic Cat's-eye. I've guarded it some thousands of years. I knew there would be a use for it at last. He may be saved yet, if some one should love him well enough to die for him."

"I do that," said the little Kitchen-Maid, and took the Cat's-eye in her hands.

"Swallow it," said the White Rat, "and you'll turn into a mouse."

The little maid swallowed it at once, and, behold! she was a little mouse.

"What am I to do?" she asked.

"I can't tell you," said the Great White Rat, "but Love will tell you."

So the little Kitchen-Maid, in the form of the mouse, ran up one of the horse's legs, and held tight on to the saddle with all her little claws.

And as the great horse galloped back towards the palace in the moonlight, she thought and thought, and at last she said to herself—

"The witch is in cat's shape, and she must have cat nature, so she will run after a mouse. She will run after *me*, and if I can lead her to a running stream she will leap across it, and then she will have to take her own shape

again. That must be what the Great
White Rat meant me to do. And if the
Cat catches me—well, at least if I can't
save my Prince I can die for him."

And the thought warmed her heart
as the great horse thundered on
through the dawnlight.

When at last, creeping softly on little
noiseless feet, the Mouse-Kitchen-Maid
re-entered the great hall, she saw that
she was only just in time, for the black
Cat was purring and looking back at the
Prince as she walked, waving her black
tail towards the further door of the hall,
and the Prince, more betwitched than
ever, was slowly following her.

Then the Real-Kitchen-Maid-
Mouse uttered a squeak, and rushed
across the porphyry floor, and the
black Cat, true to its cat nature, left
purring at the Prince and sprang after
the Mouse, and the Mouse at its best

speed, made for the garden where ran the stream that fed the marble basins where the royal gold-fish lived. The Prince understood nothing save that the enchanting black furry creature was leaving him, and in an instant he was alone. He followed to the door, and saw the Cat springing along the passage down the stairs—he followed fast—then along another passage that passed the foot of the back stairs, and he saw that the back stairs were like a water-fall—water was running down in a torrent and meandering away down the brick passage and out into the faint new sunshine.

When the Mouse saw this stream, she thought, "I'm saved." She never thought of wondering how a stream came to be running down the back stairs of the palace. When she came to think of it afterwards she always believed that the Great White Rat had managed it somehow. She never knew that it was really a great flood from the royal bathroom, where the royal housemaid, in her eagerness to run away from the witch, had left all the royal bath-taps full on.

The Mouse bounded across the stream—the Cat saw the danger, but she could not stop herself. She, too, crossed the stream, and as she crossed it she turned into the wicked fairy Malevola—cobwebs, and snakes, and newts, and bat's-wings, and all.

The Prince put his hand to his head like one awakening from sleep, and the horrible fairy vanished suddenly and for ever.

Then the Mouse ran trembling to the Prince, and in its thin little mouse's voice told him all.

"My love and my lady," he said,

holding the Mouse against his cheek. "I will marry you now. That will carry out the wicked fairy's prophecy. Then we will go back to the Great White Rat, and you shall be changed into a Princess."

So the Prince rang the church bells till all the people came out of their holes where they had been hiding, to see the strange spectacle of a Prince married to a Mouse.

And directly they were married they set off on the black charger, and when they reached the Great White Rat they told their tale.

"And now," said the Prince joyously, "if you will change her into a lady again we will go home at once and begin living happily ever after."

The Great White Rat looked at them gravely.

"It's impossible," he said. "I am

sorry, but the effects of the Magic Cat's-eye are *permanent*. Once a mouse, always a mouse, if you get moused by the Magic Cat's-eye."

The Prince and the Mouse looked sadly at each other. This was the last thing they had expected. The Great White Rat looked at them earnestly. Then he said—

"If it would be of any use to you, I've got another Magic Cat's-eye."

He held it out. The Prince took it gladly. Kingdom and the life of a king were nothing to him compared with the love and happiness of a Real-Kitchen-Maid disguised as a mouse. He put the stone to his lips.

"You know what'll happen if you do," said the Great White Rat.

"I shall change into a mouse and live happy ever after," said the Prince gaily.

"Perhaps," said the Great White Rat, "nothing is impossible if people love each other enough."

"You mustn't," cried the Mouse, trying to get between his lips and the Cat's-eye.

"My dear little Real Kitchen-Maid," said the Prince tenderly, "you have saved my life—and you *are* my life. I would rather be a mouse with you than a king without you!" And with that he swallowed the Cat's-eye, and two small mice stood side by side before the Great White Rat. Very kindly he looked at them. Then he pulled a hair from his left whisker and laid it across their little brown backs. And on the instant there stood up a Prince and a Princess and at their feet lay the little empty mouse-skins.

"It's lucky for you," said the Great White Rat, "that you chose to swal-

There stood up a prince and a princess.

low the Cat's-eye, because people who have been moused by that means can never be un-moused except *in pairs*. Nothing is impossible if people only love each other enough."

So the Prince and his bride returned to the palace and lived happy ever after. They were as happy as if they had been mice—which, in a country where there are no cats, is saying a good deal. Of course the Prince is still afraid of cats. But the curious thing is that now his wife is afraid of them too. Perhaps she learnt that lesson when she was a mouse for his sake. He, when he was a mouse for hers, learned this lesson, which is also the moral of this story: "Nothing is impossible if people only love each other enough."

✦✧✦

Melisande

OR LONG AND SHORT DIVISION

WHEN the Princess Melisande was born, her mother, the Queen, wished to have a christening party, but the King put his foot down and said he would not have it.

"I've seen too much trouble come of christening parties," said he. "However carefully you keep your visiting-book, some fairy or other is sure to get left out, and you know what *that* leads to. Why, even in my own family, the most shocking things have occurred. The Fairy Malevola was not asked to

my great-grandmother's christening—
and you know all about the spindle
and the hundred years' sleep."

"Perhaps you're right," said the
Queen. "My own cousin by marriage
forgot some stuffy old fairy or other
when she was sending out the cards
for her daughter's christening, and the
old wretch turned up at the last moment, and the girl drops toads out of
her mouth to this day."

"Just so. And then there was that
business of the mouse and the kitchen-
maids," said the King; "we'll have no
nonsense about it. I'll be her godfa-
ther, and you shall be her godmother,
and we won't ask a single fairy; then
none of them can be offended."

"Unless they all are," said the
Queen.

And that was exactly what happened. When the King and the Queen

and the baby got back from the christening the parlourmaid met them at the door, and said—

"Please, your Majesty, several ladies have called. I told them you were not at home, but they all said they'd wait."

"Are they in the parlour?" asked the Queen.

"I've shown them into the Throne Room, your Majesty," said the parlourmaid. "You see, there are several of them."

There were about seven hundred. The great Throne Room was crammed with fairies, of all ages and of all degrees of beauty and ugliness—good fairies and bad fairies, flower fairies and moon fairies, fairies like spiders and fairies like butterflies—and as the Queen opened the door and began to say how sorry she was to have kept them waiting, they all cried, with one voice, "Why didn't you ask *me* to your christening party?"

"I haven't had a party," said the Queen, and she turned to the King and whispered, "I told you so." This was her only consolation.

"You've had a christening," said the fairies, all together.

"I'm very sorry," said the poor Queen, but Malevola pushed forward and said, "Hold your tongue," most rudely.

Malevola is the oldest, as well as the most wicked, of the fairies. She is deservedly unpopular, and has been left out of more christening parties than all the rest of the fairies put together.

"Don't begin to make excuses," she said, shaking her finger at the Queen. "That only makes your conduct worse. You know well enough what happens if a fairy is left out of a christening party. We are all going to give our christening presents *now*. As the fairy of highest position, I shall begin. The Princess shall be bald."

The Queen nearly fainted as Malevola drew back, and another fairy, in a smart bonnet with snakes in it, stepped forward with a rustle of bats' wings. But the King stepped forward too.

"No you don't!" said he. "I wonder at you, ladies, I do indeed. How can you be so unfairylike? Have none of you been to school—have none of you studied the history of your own race? Surely you don't need a poor, ignorant King like me to tell you that this is *no go?*"

"How dare you?" cried the fairy in the bonnet, and the snakes in it quivered as she tossed her head. "It is my turn, and I say the Princess shall be—"

The King actually put his hand over her mouth.

"Look here," he said; "I won't have it. Listen to reason—or you'll be sorry afterwards. A fairy who breaks the traditions of fairy history goes out—you know she does—like the flame of a candle. And all tradition shows that only *one* bad fairy is ever forgotten at a christening party and the good ones are always invited; so either this is not a christening party, or else you were all invited except one, and, by her own showing, that was Malevola. It nearly always is. Do I make myself clear?"

Several of the better-class fairies who had been led away by Malevola's influence murmured that there was something in what His Majesty said.

"Try it, if you don't believe me," said the King; "give your nasty gifts to my innocent child—but as sure as you do, out you go, like a candle-flame. Now, then, will you risk it?"

No one answered, and presently several fairies came up to the Queen and said what a pleasant party it had been, but they really must be going. This example decided the rest. One by one all the fairies said good-bye and thanked the Queen for the delightful afternoon they had spent with her.

"It's been quite too lovely," said the lady with the snake-bonnet; "*do* ask us again soon, dear Queen. I shall be so *longing* to see you again, and the *dear* baby," and off she went, with the snake-trimming quivering more than ever.

When the very last fairy was gone the Queen ran to look at the baby— she tore off its Honiton lace cap and burst into tears. For all the baby's downy golden hair came off with the cap, and the Princess Melisande was as bald as an egg.

"Don't cry, my love," said the King. "I have a wish lying by, which I've never had occasion to use. My fairy godmother gave it me for a wedding present, but since then I've had nothing to wish for!"

"Thank you, dear," said the Queen, smiling through her tears.

"I'll keep the wish till baby grows up," the King went on. "And then I'll give it to her, and if she likes to wish for hair she can."

"Oh, won't you wish for it _now?_" said the Queen, dropping mixed tears and kisses on the baby's round, smooth head.

"No, dearest. She may want something else more when she grows up. And besides, her hair may grow by itself."

But it never did. Princess Melisande grew up as beautiful as the sun and as good as gold, but never a hair grew on that little head of hers. The Queen sewed her little caps of green silk, and the Princess's pink and white face looked out of these like a flower peeping out of its bud. And every day as she grew older she grew dearer, and as she grew dearer she grew better, and as she grew more good she grew more beautiful.

Now, when she was grown up the Queen said to the King—

"My love, our dear daughter is old enough to know what she wants. Let her have the wish."

So the King wrote to his fairy godmother and sent the letter by a butterfly. He asked if he might hand on to his daughter the wish the fairy had given him for a wedding present.

"I have never had occasion to use it," said he, "though it has always made me happy to remember that I had such a thing in the house. The wish is as good as new, and my daughter is now of an age to appreciate so valuable a present."

To which the fairy replied by return of butterfly:—

"Dear King,—Pray do whatever you like with my poor little present. I had quite forgotten it, but I am pleased to think that you have treasured my humble keepsake all these years.

"Your affectionate godmother,

"Fortuna F."

So the King unlocked his gold safe with the seven diamond-handled keys that hung at his girdle, and took out the wish and gave it to his daughter.

And Melisande said: "Father, I will wish that all your subjects should be quite happy.'

But they were that already, because the King and Queen were so good. So the wish did not go off.

So then she said: "Then I wish them all to be good."

But they were that already, because they were happy. So again the wish hung fire.

Then the Queen said: "Dearest, for my sake, wish what I tell you."

"Why, of course I will," said Melisande. The Queen whispered in her ear, and Melisande nodded. Then she said, aloud—

"I wish I had golden hair a yard long, and that it would grow an inch every day, and grow twice as fast every time it was cut, and—"

"Stop," cried the King. And the wish went off, and the next moment the Princess stood smiling at him through a shower of golden hair.

"Oh, how lovely," said the Queen. "What a pity you interrupted her, dear; she hadn't finished."

"What was the end?" asked the King.

"Oh," said Melisande, "I was only going to say, 'and twice as thick.' "

"It's a very good thing you didn't," said the King. "You've done about enough." For he had a mathematical mind, and could do the sums about the grains of wheat on the chess-board, and the nails in the horse's shoes, in his Royal head without any trouble at all.

"Why, what's the matter?" asked the Queen.

"You'll know soon enough," said the King. "Come, let's be happy while we may. Give me a kiss, little Melisande, and then go to nurse and ask her to teach you how to comb your hair."

"I know," said Melisande, "I've often combed mother's."

"Your mother has beautiful hair," said the King; "but I fancy you will find your own less easy to manage."

And, indeed, it was so. The Princess's hair began by being a yard long, and it grew an inch every night. If you know anything at all about the simplest sums you will see that in about five weeks her hair was about two yards long. This is a very inconvenient length. It trails on the floor and sweeps up all the dust, and though in palaces, of course, it is all gold-dust, still it is not nice to have it in your hair. And the Princess's hair was growing an inch every night. When it was three yards long the Princess could not bear it any longer—it was so heavy and so hot—so she borrowed nurse's cutting-out scissors and cut it all off, and then for a few hours she was comfortable. But the hair went on growing, and now it grew twice as fast as before; so that in thirty-six days it was as long as ever. The poor Princess cried with tiredness; when she couldn't bear it any more she cut her hair and was comfortable for a very little time. For the hair now grew four times as fast as at first, and in eighteen days it was as long as before, and she had to have it cut. Then it grew eight inches a day, and the next time it was cut it grew sixteen inches a day, and then thirty-two inches and sixty-four inches and a hundred and twenty-eight inches a day, and so on, growing twice as fast after each cutting, till the Princess would go to bed at night with her hair clipped short, and wake up in the morning with yards and yards and yards of golden hair flowing all about the room, so that she could not move without pulling her own hair, and nurse had to come and cut the hair off before she could get out of bed.

"I wish I was bald again," sighed poor Melisande, looking at the little green caps she used to wear, and she cried herself to sleep o' nights between the golden billows of the golden hair. But she never let her mother see her cry, because it was the Queen's fault, and Melisande did not want to seem to reproach her.

When first the Princess's hair grew

her mother sent locks of it to all her Royal relations, who had them set in rings and brooches. Later, the Queen was able to send enough for bracelets and girdles. But presently so much hair was cut off that they had to burn it. Then when autumn came all the crops failed; it seemed as though all the gold of harvest had gone into the Princess's hair. And there was a famine. Then Melisande said—

"It seems a pity to waste all my hair; it does grow so very fast. Couldn't we stuff things with it, or something, and sell them, to feed the people?"

So the King called a council of merchants, and they sent out samples of the Princess's hair, and soon orders came pouring in; and the Princess's hair became the staple export of that country. They stuffed pillows with it, and they stuffed beds with it. They made ropes of it for sailors to use, and curtains for hanging in Kings' palaces. They made haircloth of it, for hermits, and other people who wished to be uncomfy. But it was so soft and silky that it only made them happy and warm, which they did not wish to be. So the hermits gave up wearing it, and, instead, mothers bought it for their little babies, and all well-born infants wore little shirts of Princess-haircloth.

And still the hair grew and grew. And the people were fed and the famine came to an end.

The the King said: "It was all very well while the famine lasted—but now I shall write to my fairy godmother and see if something cannot be done."

So he wrote and sent the letter by a skylark, and by return of bird came this answer—

"Why not advertise for a competent Prince? Offer the usual reward."

So the King sent out his heralds all over the world to proclaim that any respectable Prince with proper references should marry the Princess Melisande if he could stop her hair growing.

Then from far and near came trains of Princes anxious to try their luck, and they brought all sorts of nasty things with them in bottles and round wooden boxes. The Princess tried all the remedies, but she did not like any of them, and she did not like any of the Princes, so in her heart she was rather glad that none of the nasty things in bottles and boxes made the least difference to her hair.

The Princess had to sleep in the great Throne Room now, because no other room was big enough to hold

*There were trains of princes bringing
nasty things in bottles and
round wooden boxes.*

her and her hair. When she woke in the morning the long high room would be quite full of her golden hair, packed tight and thick like wool in a barn. And every night when she had had the hair cut close to her head she would sit in her green silk gown by the window and cry, and kiss the little green caps she used to wear, and wish herself bald again.

It was as she sat crying there on Midsummer Eve that she first saw Prince Florizel.

He had come to the palace that evening, but he would not appear in her presence with the dust of travel on him, and she had retired with her hair borne by twenty pages before he had bathed and changed his garments and entered the reception-room.

Now he was walking in the garden in the moonlight, and he looked up and she looked down, and for the first time Melisande, looking on a Prince, wished that he might have the power to stop her hair from growing. As for the Prince, he wished many things, and the first was granted him. For he said—

"You are Melisande?"

"And you are Florizel?"

"There are many roses round your window,' said he to her, "and none down here."

She threw him one of three white roses she held in her hand. Then he said—

"White rose trees are strong. May I climb up to you?"

"Surely," said the Princess.

So he climbed up to the window.

"Now," he said, "if I can do what your father asks, will you marry me?"

"My father has promised that I

shall," said Melisande, playing with the white roses in her hand.

"Dear Princess," said he, "your father's promise is nothing to me. I want yours. Will you give it to me?"

"Yes," said she, and gave him the second rose.

"I want your hand."

"Yes," she said.

"And your heart with it."

"Yes," said the Princess, and she gave him the third rose.

"And a kiss to seal the promise."

"Yes," said she.

"And a kiss to go with the hand."

"Yes," she said.

"And a kiss to bring the heart."

"Yes," said the Princess, and she gave him the three kisses.

"Now," said he, when he had given them back to her, "to-night do not go to bed. Stay by your window, and I will stay down here in the garden and watch. And when your hair has grown to the filling of your room call to me, and then do as I tell you."

"I will," said the Princess.

So at dewy sunrise the Prince, lying on the turf beside the sun-dial, heard her voice—

"Florizel! Florizel! My hair has grown so long that it is pushing me out of the window."

"Get out on to the window-sill," said he, "and twist your hair three times round the great iron hook that is there."

And she did.

Then the Prince climbed up the rose bush with his naked sword in his teeth, and he took the Princess's hair in his hand about a yard from her head and said—

"Jump!"

The Princess jumped, and screamed, for there she was hanging from the hook by a yard and a half of her bright hair; the Prince tightened his grasp of the hair and drew his sword across it.

Then he let her down gently by her hair till her feet were on the grass, and jumped down after her.

They stayed talking in the garden till all the shadows had crept under their proper trees and the sun-dial said it was breakfast time.

Then they went in to breakfast, and all the Court crowded round to wonder and admire. For the Princess's hair had not grown.

"How did you do it?" asked the King, shaking Florizel warmly by the hand.

"The simplest thing in the world," said Florizel, modestly. "You have always cut the hair off the Princess. *I* just cut the Princess off the hair."

"Humph!" said the King, who had a logical mind. And during breakfast he more than once looked anxiously at his daughter. When they got up from breakfast the Princess rose with the rest, but she rose and rose and rose, till it seemed as though there would never be an end of it. The Princess was nine feet high.

"I feared as much," said the King, sadly. "I wonder what will be the rate of progression. You see," he said to poor Florizel, "when we cut the hair off *it* grows—when we cut the Princess off *she* grows. I wish you had happened to think of that!"

The Princess went on growing. By dinner-time she was so large that she had to have her dinner brought out into the garden because she was too large to get indoors. But she was too unhappy to be able to eat anything. And she cried so much that there was quite a pool in the garden, and several pages were nearly drowned. So she remembered her "Alice in Wonderland," and stopped crying at once. But she did not stop growing. She grew bigger and bigger and bigger, till she had to go outside the palace gardens and sit on the common, and even that was too small to hold her comfortably, for every hour she grew twice as much as she had done the hour before. And nobody knew what to do, nor where the Princess was to sleep. Fortunately, her clothes had grown with her, or she would have been very cold indeed, and now she sat on the common in her green gown, embroidered with gold, looking like a great hill covered with gorse in flower.

The princess grew so big that she had to go and sit on the common.

You cannot possibly imagine how large the Princess was growing, and her mother stood wringing her hands on the castle tower, and the Prince Florizel looked on broken-hearted to see his Princess snatched from his arms and turned into a lady as big as a mountain.

The King did not weep or look on. He sat down at once and wrote to his fairy godmother, asking her advice. He sent a weasel with the letter, and by return of weasel he got his own letter back again, marked "Gone away. Left no address."

It was now, when the kingdom was plunged into gloom, that a neighbouring King took it into his head to send an invading army against the island where Melisande lived. They came in ships and they landed in great numbers, and Melisande looking down from her height saw alien soldiers marching on the sacred soil of her country.

"I don't mind so much now," said she, "if I can really be of some use this size."

And she picked up the army of the enemy in handfuls and double-handfuls, and put them back into their ships, and gave a little flip to each transport ship with her finger and thumb, which sent the ships off so fast that they never stopped til they reached their own country, and when they arrived there the whole army to a man said it would rather be court-martialled a hundred times over than go near the place again.

Meantime Melisande, sitting on the highest hill on the island, felt the land trembling and shivering under her giant feet.

"I do believe I'm getting too heavy," she said, and jumped off the island into the sea, which was just up to her ankles. Just then a great fleet of warships and gunboats and torpedo boats came in sight, on their way to attack the island.

Melisande could easily have sunk them all with one kick, but she did not like to do this because it might have drowned the sailors, and besides, it might have swamped the island.

So she simply stooped and picked the island as you would pick a mushroom—for, of course, all islands are supported by a stalk underneath—and carried it away to another part of the world. So that when the warships got to where the island was marked on the map they found nothing but sea, and a very rough sea it was, because the Princess had churned it all up with her

ankles as she walked away through it
with the island.

When Melisande reached a suitable
place, very sunny and warm, and with
no sharks in the water, she set down
the island; and the people made it fast
with anchors, and then every one
went to bed, thanking the kind fate
which had sent them so great a Princess to help them in their need, and
calling her the saviour of her country
and the bulwark of the nation.

But it is poor work being the nation's bulwark and your country's saviour when you are miles high, and
have no one to talk to, and when all
you want is to be your humble right
size again and to marry your sweetheart. And when it was dark the Princess came close to the island, and
looked down, from far up, at her palace and her tower and cried, and cried,

and cried. It does not matter how much you cry into the sea, it hardly makes any difference, however large you may be. Then when everything was quite dark the Princess looked up at the stars.

"I wonder how soon I shall be big enough to knock my head against them," said she.

And as she stood star-gazing she heard a whisper right in her ear. A very little whisper, but quite plain.

"Cut off your hair!" it said.

Now, everything the Princess was wearing had grown big along with her, so that now there dangled from her golden girdle a pair of scissors as big as the Malay Peninsula, together with a pin-cushion the size of the Isle of Wight, and a yard measure that would have gone round Australia.

And when she heard the little, little

voice, she knew it, small as it was, for the dear voice of Prince Florizel, and she whipped out the scissors from her gold case and snip, snip, snipped all her hair off, and it fell into the sea. The coral insects got hold of it at once and set to work on it, and now they have made it into the biggest coral reef in the world; but that has nothing to do with the story.

Then the voice said, "Get close to the island," and the Princess did, but she could not get very close because she was so large, and she looked up again at the stars and they seemed to be much farther off.

Then the voice said, "Be ready to swim," and she felt something climb out of her ear and clamber down her arm. The stars got farther and farther away, and next moment the Princess found herself swimming in the sea, and Prince Florizel swimming beside her.

"I crept on to your hand when you were carrying the island," he explained, when their feet touched the sand and they walked in through the shallow water, "and I got into your ear with an ear-trumpet. You never noticed me because you were so great then."

"Oh, my dear Prince," cried Melisande, falling into his arms, "you have saved me. I am my proper size again."

So they went home and told the King and Queen. Both were very, very happy, but the King rubbed his chin with his hand, and said—

"You've certainly had some fun for your money, young man, but don't you see that we're just where we were before? Why, the child's hair is growing already."

And indeed it was.

Then once more the King sent a letter to his godmother. He sent it by a flying-fish, and by return of fish come the answer—

"Just back from my holidays. Sorry for your troubles. Why not try scales?"

And on this message the whole Court pondered for weeks.

But the Prince caused a pair of gold scales to be made, and hung them up in the palace gardens under a big oak tree. And one morning he said to the Princess—

"My darling Melisande, I must really speak seriously to you. We are getting on in life. I am nearly twenty: it is time that we thought of being settled. Will you trust me entirely and get into one of those gold scales?"

So he took her down into the garden, and helped her into the scale, and she curled up in it in her green and gold gown, like a little grass mound with buttercups on it.

"And what is going into the other scale?" asked Melisande.

"Your hair," said Florizel. "You see, when your hair is cut off you it grows, and when you are cut off your hair you grow—oh, my heart's delight, I can never forget how you grew, never! But if, when your hair is no more than you, and you are no more than your hair, I snip the scissors between you and it, then neither you nor your hair can possibly decide which ought to go on growing."

"Suppose *both* did," said the poor Princess, humbly.

"Impossible," said the Prince, with a shudder; "there are limits even to Malevola's malevolence. And, besides, Fortuna said 'Scales.' Will you try it?"

"I will do whatever you wish," said the poor Princess, "but let me kiss my father and mother once, and Nurse, and you, too, my dear, in case I grow large again and can kiss nobody any more."

So they came one by one and kissed the Princess.

Then the nurse cut off the Princess's hair, and at once it began to grow at a frightful rate.

The King and Queen and nurse busily packed it, as it grew, into the other scale, and gradually the scale went down a little. The Prince stood waiting between the scales with his drawn sword, and just before the two were equal he struck. But during the time his sword took to flash through the air the Princess's hair grew a yard or two, so that at the instant when he struck the balance was true.

"You are a young man of sound

*The princess was in one scale and
her hair in the other.*

judgment," said the King, embracing him, while the Queen and the nurse ran to help the Princess out of the gold scale.

The scale full of golden hair bumped down on to the ground as the Princess stepped out of the other one, and stood there before those who loved her, laughing and crying with happiness, because she remained her proper size, and her hair was not growing any more.

She kissed her Prince a hundred times, and the very next day they were married. Every one remarked on the beauty of the bride, and it was noticed that her hair was quite short—only five feet five and a quarter inches long—just down to her pretty ankles. Because the scales had been ten feet ten and a half inches apart, and the Prince, having a straight eye, had cut the golden hair exactly in the middle!

The Town in the Library in the Town in the Library

ROSAMUND and Fabian were left alone in the library. You may not believe this; but I advise you to believe everything I tell you, because it is true. Truth is stranger than story-books, and when you grow up you will hear people say this till you grow quite sick of listening to them: you will then want to write the strangest story that ever was—just to show that *some* stories can be stranger than truth.

Mother was obliged to leave the children alone, because Nurse was ill with measles, which seems a babyish thing for a grown-up nurse to have—but it is quite true. If I had wanted to make up anything I could have said she was ill of a broken heart or a brain-fever, which always happens in books. But I wish to speak the truth even if it sounds silly. And it *was* measles.

Mother could not stay with the children, because it was Christmas Eve, and on that day a lot of poor old people came up to get their Christmas presents, tea and snuff, and flannel petticoats, and warm capes, and boxes of needles and cottons and things like that. Generally the children helped to give out the presents, but this year Mother was afraid they might be going to have measles themselves, and measles is a nasty forward illness with no manners at all. You can catch it from a person before they know they've got it, and if Rosamund and Fabian had been going to have it they might have given it to all the old men and women who came up to get their Christmas presents. And measles is a present no old men or women want to have given them, even at Christmas time, no matter how old they may be. They would not mind brain-fever or a broken heart so much perhaps—because it is more interesting. But no one can think it interesting to have measles, at any rate till you come to the part where they give you jelly and boiled sole.

So the children were left alone. Before Mother went away she said—

"Look here, dears, you may play with your bricks, or make pictures with your pretty blocks that kind Uncle Thomas gave you, but you must not touch the two top-drawers of the bureau. Now don't forget. And if you're good you shall have tea with me, and perhaps there will be cake. Now you *will* be good, won't you?"

Fabian and Rosamund promised faithfully that they would be *very* good and that they would not touch the two top-drawers, and Mother went away to see about the flannel petticoats and the tea and snuff and tobacco and things. When the children were left alone, Fabian said—

"I am going to be very good, I shall be much more good than Mother expects me to."

"We *won't* look in the drawers," said Rosamund, stroking the shiny top of the bureau.

"We won't even *think* about the insides of the drawers," said Fabian. He stroked the bureau too and his fingers left four long streaks on it, because he had been eating toffee.

"I suppose," he said presently, "we may open the two *bottom* drawers? Mother couldn't have made a mistake—could she?"

So they opened the two bottom drawers just to be sure that Mother hadn't made a mistake, and to see whether there was anything in the bottom drawers that they ought not to look at.

But the bottom drawer of all had only old magazines in it. And the next to the bottom drawer had a lot of papers in it. The children knew at once by the look of the papers that they belonged to Father's great work about the Domestic Life of the Ancient Druids, and they knew it was not right— or even interesting—to try to read other people's papers.

So they shut the drawers and looked
at each other, and Fabian said, "I think
it would be right to play with the
bricks and the pretty blocks that Uncle
Thomas gave us."

But Rosamund was younger than
Fabian, and she said, "I am tired of the
blocks, and I am tired of Uncle
Thomas. I would rather look in the
drawers."

"So would I," said Fabian. And
they stood looking at the bureau.

Perhaps you don't know what a bureau is—children learn very little at
school nowadays—so I will tell you
that a bureau is a kind of chest of
drawers. Sometimes it has a bookcase
on the top of it, and instead of the two
little top corner drawers like the chests
of drawers in a bedroom it has a slop-
ing lid, and when it is quite open you
pull out two little boards under-

neath—and then it makes a sort of shelf for people to write letters on. The shelf lies quite flat, and lets you see little drawers inside with mother of pearl handles—and a row of pigeon holes—(which are not holes pigeons live in, but places for keeping the letters carrier-pigeons could carry round their necks if they liked). And there is very often a tiny cupboard in the middle of the bureau, with a pattern on the door in different coloured woods. So now you know.

Fabian stood first on one leg and then on the other, till Rosamund said—

"Well, you might as well pull up your stockings."

So he did. His stockings were always just like a concertina or a very expensive photographic camera, but he used to say it was not his fault, and

I suppose he knew best. Then he said—

"I say, Rom! mother only said we weren't to *touch* the two top-drawers—"

"I *should* like to be good," said Rosamund.

"I *mean* to be good," said Fabian. "But if you took the little thin poker that is not kept for best you could put it through one of the brass handles and I could hold the other handle with the tongs. And then we could open the drawer without touching it."

"So we could! How clever you are, Fabe," said Rosamund. And she admired her brother very much. So they took the poker and the tongs. The front of the bureau got a little scratched, but the top drawer came open, and there they saw two boxes with glass tops and narrow gold paper going all round; though you could only see paper shavings through the glass they knew it was soldiers. Besides these boxes there was a doll and a donkey standing on a green grass plot that had wooden wheels, and a little wicker-work doll's cradle, and some brass cannons, and a bag that looked like marbles, and some flags, and a mouse that seemed as though it moved with clockwork; only, of course, they had promised not to touch the drawer, so they could not make sure. There was a wooden box, too, and it was wrong way up and on the bottom of it was written in pencil, "Vill: and anim: 5/9½." They looked at each other, and Fabian said:

"I wish it was to-morrow!"

You have seen that Fabian was quite a clever boy; and he knew at once that these were the Christmas presents which Santa Claus had brought for him and Rosamund. But Rosamund said, "Oh dear, I wish we hadn't!"

However, she consented to open the other drawer—without touching it, of course, because she had promised faithfully—and when, with the poker and tongs, the other drawer came open, there were large wooden boxes—the kind that hold raisins and figs—and round boxes with paper on—smooth on the top and folded in pleats round the edge; and the children knew what was inside without looking. Every one knows what candied fruit looks like on the outside of the box. There were square boxes, too— the kind that have crackers in—with a cracker going off on the lid, very different in size and brightness from what it really does, for, as no doubt you know, a cracker very often comes in two quite calmly, without any pop at all, and then you only have the motto and the sweet, which is never nice. Of course, if there is anything else in the cracker, such as brooches or rings, you have to let the little girl who sits next to you at supper have it.

When they had pushed back the drawer Fabian said—

"Let us pull out the writing drawer and make a castle."

So they pulled the drawer out and put it on the floor. Please do not try to do this if your father has a bureau, because it leads to trouble. It was only because this one was broken that they were able to do it.

Then they began to build. They had the two boxes of bricks—the wooden bricks with the pillars and the coloured glass windows, and the rational bricks which are made of clay like tiles, and

their father called them the All-Wool
bricks, which seems silly, only of
course grown-up people always talk
sense. When all the bricks were used
up they got the pretty picture blocks
that kind Uncle Thomas gave them,
and they built with these; but one box
of blocks does not go far. Picture
blocks are only good for building, except just at first. When you have made
the pictures a few times you know exactly how they go, and then what's the
good? This is a fault which belongs to
many very expensive toys. These
blocks had six pictures—Windsor Castle with the Royal Standard hoisted;
ducks in a pond, with a very handsome green and blue drake; Rebecca
at the well; a snowball fight—but
none of the boys knew how to chuck
a snowball; the Harvest Home; and
the Death of Nelson.

These did not go far, as I said. There are six times as few blocks as there are pictures, because every block has six sides. If you don't understand this it shows they don't teach arithmetic at your school, or else that you don't do your home lessons.

But the best of a library is the books. Rosamund and Fabian made up with books. They got Shakespeare in fourteen volumes, and Rollin's "Ancient History," and Gibbon's "Decline and Fall," and "The Beauties of Literature" on fifty-six fat little volumes, and they built not only a castle, but a town—and a big town—that presently towered high above them at the top of the bureau.

"It's almost big enough to get into," said Fabian, "if we had some steps." So they made steps with the "British Essayists," the "Spectator," and the "Rambler," and the "Observer," and the "Tatler"; and when the steps were done they walked up them.

You may think that they could not have walked up these steps and into a town they had built themselves, but I assure you people have often done it, and anyway this is a true story. They had made a lovely gateway with two fat volumes of Macaulay and Milton's poetical works on top, and as they went through it they felt all the feelings which people have to feel when they are tourists and see really fine architecture. (Architecture means buildings, but it is a grander word, as you see.)

Rosamund and Fabian simply walked up the steps into the town they had built. Whether they got larger or the town got smaller, I do not pretend to say. When they had gone under the great gateway they found that they were in a street which they could not remember building. But they were not disagreeable about it, and they said it was a very nice street all the same.

There was a large square in the middle of the town, with seats, and there they sat down, in the town they had made, and wondered how they could have been so clever as to build it. Then they went to the walls of the town—high, strong walls built of the Encyclopedia and the Biographical Dictionary—and far away over the brown plain of the carpet they saw a great thing like a square mountain. It was very shiny. And as they looked at it a great slice of it pushed itself out, and Fabian saw the brass handles shine, and he said:

"Why, Rom, that's the bureau."

"It's larger than I want it to be," said Rosamund, who was a little frightened. And indeed it did seem to be an extra size, for it was higher than the town.

The drawer of the great mountain bureau opened slowly, and the children could see something moving inside; then they saw the glass lid of one of the boxes go slowly up till it stood on end and looked like one side of the Crystal Palace, it was so large—and inside the box they saw something moving. The shavings and tissue-paper and the cotton-wool heaved and tossed like a sea when it is rough and you wish you had not come for a sail. And then from among the heaving whiteness came out a blue soldier, and another and another. They let themselves down from the drawer with ropes of shavings, and when they were all out there were fifty of them—foot soldiers with rifles and fixed bayonets, as well as a thin captain on a horse and a sergeant and a drummer.

The drummer beat his drum and the whole company formed fours and marched straight for the town. They seemed to be quite full-size soldiers—indeed, *extra* large.

The children were very frightened. They left the walls and ran up and down the streets of the town trying to find a place to hide.

"Oh, there's our very own house," cried Rosamund at last; "we shall be safe there." She was surprised as well as pleased to find their own house inside the town they had built.

So they ran in, and into the library, and there was the bureau and the castle they had built, and it was all small and quite the proper size. But when

they looked out of the window it was
not their own street, but the one they
had built; they could see two volumes
of the "Beauties of Literature" and the
head of Rebecca in the house opposite, and down the street was the Mausoleum they had built after the pattern
given in the red and yellow book that
goes with the All-Wool bricks. It was
all very confusing.

Suddenly, as they stood looking out
of the windows, they heard a shout-
ing, and there were the blue soldiers
coming along the street by twos, and
when the Captain got opposite their
house he called out—

"Fabian! Rosamund! come down!"

And they had to, for they were very
much frightened.

Then the Captain said—

"We have taken this town, and you
are our prisoners. Do not attempt to

escape, or I don't know what will happen to you."

The children explained that they
had built the town, so they thought it
was theirs; but the captain said very
politely—

"That doesn't follow at all. It's our
town now. And I want provisions for
my soldiers."

"We haven't any," said Fabian, but
Rosamund nudged him, and said,
"Won't the soldiers be very fierce if
they are hungry?"

The Blue Captain heard her, and
said—

"You are quite right, little girl. If
you have any food, produce it. It will
be a generous act, and may stop any
unpleasantness. My soldiers *are* very
fierce. Besides," he added in a lower
tone, speaking behind his hand, "you

need only feed the soldiers in the usual way."

When the children heard this their minds were made up.

"If you do not mind waiting a minute," said Fabian, politely, "I will bring down any little things I can find."

Then he took his tongs, and Rosamund took the poker, and they opened the drawer where the raisins and figs and dried fruits were—for everything in the library in the town was just the same as in the library at home—and they carried them out into the big square where the Captain had drawn up his blue regiment. And here the soldiers were fed. I suppose you know how tin soldiers are fed? But children learn so little at school nowadays that I daresay you don't, so I will tell you. You just put a bit of the fig or raisin, or whatever it is, on the soldier's tin bayonet—or his sword, if he is a cavalry man—and you let it stay on till you are tired of playing at giving the soldiers rations, and then of course *you eat it for him.* This was the way in which Fabian and Rosamund fed the starving blue soldiers. But when they had done so, the soldiers were as hungry as ever. Which only shows that soldiers are an ungrateful lot, and it is idle to try and make their lives better and brighter.

So then the Blue Captain, who had not had anything, even on the point of his sword, said—

"More—more, my gallant men are fainting for lack of food."

So there was nothing for it but to bring out the candied fruits, and to feed the soldiers with them. So Fabian and Rosamund stuck bits of candied apricot and fig and pear and cherry and beetroot on the tops of the soldiers' bayonets, and when every soldier had a piece they put a fat candied cherry on the officer's sword. Then the children knew the soldiers would be quiet for a few minutes, and they ran back into their own house and into the library to talk to each other about what they had better do, for they both felt that the blue soldiers were a very hard-hearted set of men.

"They might shut us up in the dungeons," said Rosamund, "and then Mother might lock us in, when she shut up the lid of the bureau, and we should starve to death."

For they could not be sure exactly what size they were, or which library their Mother would come back to when she had given away all the flannel petticoats and things.

The dungeons were the pigeon-
holes of the bureau, and the doors of
them were the little "Beauties of Literature"—very heavy doors they were
too.

You see the curious thing was that
the children had built a town and got
into it, and in it they had found their
own house with the very town they
had built—or one exactly like it—still
on the library floor.

"I think it's all nonsense," said Rosamund. But when they looked out of
the window there was the house with
Windsor Castle and the head of Rebecca just opposite.

"If we could only find Mother," she
said; but they knew without looking
that Mother was not in the house that
they were in then.

"I wish we had that mouse that
looked like clockwork—and the don-

key, and the other box of soldiers—
perhaps they are red ones, and they
would fight the blue and lick them—
because red-coats are English and they
always win," said Fabian.

And then Rosamund said—

"Oh, Fabe, I believe we could go
into *this* town, too, if we tried! Let us
put all the things in, and then try!"

So they went to the bureau drawer,
and Rosamund got out the other box
of soldiers and the mouse—it *was* a
clockwork one—and the donkey with
panniers, and put them in the town,
while Fabian ate up a few odd raisins
that had dropped on the floor.

When all the soldiers (they *were* red)
were arranged on the ramparts of the
little town, Fabian said—

"I am thinking of all the raisins and
things on the soldiers' bayonets out-

side. It seems a pity not to eat the things for them."

But Rosamund said—

"No, no; let's get into this town, and perhaps we shall be safe from the blue soldiers. Oh, Fabe, never mind the raisins!"

But Fabian said, "I don't want you to come if you're frightened. I'll go alone. Who's afraid?"

So then of course Rosamund said she would come with him, so they went out and ate the things for the soldiers, leaving the Captain's cherry for the last. And when that was eaten they ran as hard as they could back to their house and into the library, where the town was on the floor, with the little red soldiers on the ramparts.

"I'm sure we can get into this town," cried Fabian, and sure enough they did, just as they had done into the first one. Whether they got smaller or the town got larger I leave you to decide. And it was exactly the same sort of town as the other. So now they were in a town built in a library in a house in a town built in a library in a house in a town called London—and the town they were in now had red soldiers in it and they felt quite safe, and the Union Jack was stuck up over the gateway. It was a stiff little flag they had found with some others in the bureau drawer; it was meant to be stuck in the Christmas pudding, but they had stuck it between two blocks and put it over the gate of their town. They walked about this town and found their own house, just as before, and went in, and there was the toy town on the floor; and you will see that they might have walked into that town also, but they saw that it was no

good, and that they couldn't get out
that way, but would only get deeper
and deeper into a nest of towns in libraries in houses in towns in libraries
in houses in towns in . . . and so on
for always—something like Chinese
puzzle-boxes multiplied by millions
and millions for ever and ever. And
they did not like even to think of this,
because of course they would be getting further and further from home
every time. And when Fabian explained all this to Rosamund she said
he made her head ache, and she began
to cry.

Then Fabian thumped her on the
back and told her not to be a little silly,
for he was a very kind brother. And he
said—

"Come out and let's see if the soldiers can tell us what to do."

So they went out; but the red soldiers

said they knew nothing but drill, and even the Red Captain said he really couldn't advise. Then they met the clockwork mouse. He was big like an elephant, and the donkey with panniers was as big as a mastodon or a mega-therium. (If they teach you anything at school of course they have taught you all about the megatherium and the mas-todon.)

The Mouse kindly stopped to speak to the children, and Rosamund burst into tears again and said she wanted to go home.

The great Mouse looked down at her and said—

"I am sorry for *you*, but your brother is the kind of child that overwinds clockwork mice the very first day he has them. I prefer to stay this size."

Then Fabian said: "On my honour, I won't. If we get back home I'll give you to Rosamund. That is, supposing I get you for one of my Christmas presents."

The donkey with panniers said—

"And you won't put coals in my panniers or unglue my feet from my green grass-plot because I look more natural without wheels?"

"I give you my word," said Fabian, "I wouldn't think of such a thing."

"Very well," said the Mouse, "then I will tell you. It is a great secret, but there is only one way to get out of this kind of town. You—I hardly know how to explain—you—you just *walk out of the gate*, you know."

"Dear me," said Rosamund; "I never thought of that!"

So they all went to the gate of the town and walked out, and there they were in the library again. But when they looked out of the window the

All-Wool Mausoleum was still to be seen, and the terrible blue soldiers.

"What are we to do now?" asked Rosamund; but the clockwork mouse and the donkey with panniers were their proper size again now (or else the children had got bigger. It is no use asking me which, for I do not know), and so of course they could not speak.

"We must walk out of this town as we did out of the other," said Fabian.

"Yes," Rosamund said; "only this town is full of blue soldiers and I am afraid of them. Don't you think it would do if we *ran* out?"

So out they ran and down the steps that were made of the "Spectator" and the "Rambler" and the "Tatler" and the "Observer." And directly they stood on the brown library carpet they ran to the window and looked out, and they saw—instead of the building with

Windsor Castle and Rebecca's head in it, and the All-Wool Mausoleum—they saw their own road with the trees without any leaves and the man was just going along lighting the lamps with the stick that the gas-light pops out of, like a bird, to roost in the glass cage at the top of the lamp-post. So they knew that they were safe at home again.

And as they stood looking out they heard the library door open, and Mother's voice saying—

"What a dreadful muddle! And what have you done with the raisins and the candied fruits?" And her voice was very grave indeed.

Now you will see that it was quite impossible for Fabian and Rosamund to explain to their mother what they had done with the raisins and things, and how they had been in a town in a library in a house in a town they had built in their own library with the books and the bricks and the pretty picture blocks kind Uncle Thomas gave them. Because they were much younger than I am, and even I have found it rather hard to explain.

So Rosamund said, "Oh, Mother, my head does ache so," and began to cry. And Fabian said nothing, but he, also, began to cry.

And Mother said, "I don't wonder your head aches, after all those sweet things." And she looked as if she would like to cry too.

"I don't know what Daddy will say," said Mother, and then she gave them each a nasty powder and put them both to bed.

"I wonder what he *will* say," said Fabian just before he went to sleep.

"*I* don't know," said Rosamund, and, strange to say, they don't know to this hour what Daddy said. Because next day they both had measles, and when they got better every one had forgotten about what had happened on Christmas Eve. And Fabian and Rosamund had forgotten just as much as everybody else. So I should never have heard of it but for the clockwork mouse. It was he who told me the story, just as the children told it to him in the town in the library in the house in the town they built in their own library with the books and the bricks and the pretty picture blocks which were given to them by kind Uncle Thomas. And if you do not believe the story it is not my fault: I believe every word the mouse said, for I know the good character of that clockwork mouse, and I know it could not tell an untruth even if it tried.

LIBRARY OF CONGRESS
CATALOGING-IN-PUBLICATION DATA

Nesbit, E. (Edith), 1858–1924.
Whereyouwantogoto and other unlikely tales/
E. Nesbit; illustrated by H. R. Millar and
Claude A. Shepperson.
p.   cm.—(Little barefoot books)
Contents: The cockatoucan—Whereyouwantogoto
—The prince, two mice, and some kitchen-maids
—Melisande—The town in the library,
in the town in the library.
ISBN 1-56957-904-0 (alk. paper)
1. Children's stories, English. [1. Fantasy.
2. Short stories.] I. Millar, H. R., ill.
II. Shepperson, Claude A., ill. III. Title.
IV. Title: Where you want to go to. V. Series.
PZ7.N43777Wh 1993   93-18685
[Fic]—dc20   CIP
                                        AC

UK edition: ISBN 1-898000-35-2
British Library Cataloguing-in-Publication data:
A copy of this title is available from The British Library

LITTLE BAREFOOT BOOKS

Alice's Adventures in Wonderland
by Lewis Carroll
Illustrated by John Tenniel

The Brownies' Merry Adventures
written and illustrated by
Palmer Cox

*How the Leopard Got His Spots
and Other Just So Stories*
by Rudyard Kipling
Illustrated by Rudyard Kipling
and Joseph M. Gleeson

The Light Princess
by George MacDonald
Illustrated by Arthur Hughes

(continued on next page)

*Whereyouwantogoto
and Other Unlikely Tales*
by E. Nesbit
Illustrated by H. R. Millar
and Claude A. Shepperson

The World Is Round
by Gertrude Stein
Illustrated by Roberta Arenson